MALCOLM

Cross and Crown - Book 2

SKYLAR WEST

Published by Blushing Books
An Imprint of
ABCD Graphics and Design, Inc.
A Virginia Corporation
977 Seminole Trail #233
Charlottesville, VA 22901

Skylar West
Malcolm

eBook ISBN: 978-1-64563-550-5
Print ISBN: 978-1-64563-582-6
v1

Chapter 1

Malcolm

Yesterday turned out much differently than anticipated, causing me to reflect on recent events as I perused the gallery in my father's estate. My father, Henry Fitzwilliam, was from a long line of Crown supporters whose origins started in Sussex, England, several hundred years ago.

I slowed my ambling to gaze into the eyes of the first Fitzwilliam, Sir William of Southampton, and peered at the long line of portraits to the current Fitzwilliam, Henry, my father. But I was not his son by birth. I had come to learn that he was my adopted father and the woman I'd called Mother, his wife.

My birth mother was now comfortably stationed in the Edinburgh Clinic, a short drive from my home. Staring into the warm eyes of my stepfather, I wondered how my life had recently become such a clusterfuck.

I plunked down on one of the many chaises and stared at

the wall of legitimate Fitzwilliam men, my mind drifting back to that fateful day not long ago when I met my mother.

The day was chilly, with a steady drizzle of rain that had been coming down all day. I rushed from the gym to my car and found a woman blocking the driver's door.

"Hello, John."

"Sorry, lady, you have the wrong man. My name is Malcolm."

She wouldn't move, but stood firmly and regarded me with an uncomfortable intensity. *"You are tall, so very tall, almost as tall as yer brother. Your father is short, and you don't look a thing like him."* She was correct in that I didn't look a thing like my father and, until recently, had never questioned it. But I didn't have a brother and was beginning to wonder if the woman was on drugs.

"You look like your real father, not that short pretender, Fitzwilliam." Her words stirred a recent memory, one of my father's best mates, Sir Robert Campbell.

I had only seen the man a few times, and something about him had struck a chord every time, although I couldn't put my finger on what exactly. Until I looked at myself in a mirror hanging on the wall outside of the den. Both men were sitting across from each other in leather armchairs.

Sir Robert's coloring was different, but his build, his posture, reminded me of myself. I looked back at him and then the mirror, the unthinkable dawning in my consciousness like a nightmare come to life.

I looked at Henry, my father, and knew that I wasn't his. It was like a bolt of understanding had hit me, and when I glanced back at his friend, Robert, I knew I was his.

"I'm yer mother, Annie. You were born John, and Sir Robert Campbell Lord of Roswell is yer father."

I stood in the drizzle, no longer feeling the cold, no longer feeling anything. "Perhaps we should talk." Maybe she was crazy. Maybe what I saw in the mirror several weeks earlier was a figment. But I needed to hear what this woman had to say regardless.

"Come, I know a place we can talk." I opened the passenger door for her and drove to a secluded spot to hear her story.

"Malcolm!" Henry came around the corner at the end of the gallery. "There you are," he said, coming to a stop in front of me. Are you ready, Malcolm, as it's time to go."

"As ready as I'll ever be," I sighed in resignation. Just yesterday, I had kidnapped my half-brother's girlfriend. Today was the first day of whatever was to come next, and I didn't know how to feel about any of it.

Henry approached me as one would an injured animal and gently placed a hand on my shoulder. "You are a good man, Malcolm, don't fret. What's done is done, and we can't fix past events, but we can move forward.

"If I could do things over again, I would. I should have talked to you when I first discovered the truth about Sir Robert. I should have seen that Annie was off her rocker, and although correct about some things, her jaded perspective was terrifying to see when she finally became unhinged. She really holds a grudge against Laughlin, and none of this is his fault."

"Aye," Henry answered, "Annie has problems, and with the other two dead, she needed someone new to take her rage out on. Regarding her jaded perspective, Laughlin has seen her every day of his life and didn't notice, either. It stands to reason that Annie must be a good actress or very ill. Regardless of how her treatment and hopefully subsequent cure goes, you still have a life to live."

"You are right again… Do I still call you Father?"

Henry's face became serious as he glared at me. "You have been and will always be my son and heir. I raised you and made you mine. Of course, you are calling me Father." I smiled at the vehemence in his tone.

"All right, no need to get American on me, da." I used my old name for him, which brought an immediate smile to his face. We left his estate for the short drive to Laughlin's castle, and as each mile brought us closer, I felt the horror of my actions more acutely. Could I face them? I didn't see how we could move forward, as kidnapping is a pretty serious crime.

We passed through the gate and drove the few hundred feet to the circular driveway. I wanted to hide when I saw Laughlin and Suri waiting for us on the steps with smiles that seemed to hold no nefarious intentions toward me. Maybe it was a trick, and they were acting as Annie had been. We'd soon find out.

Henry embraced Laughlin and took a moment to properly greet Suri, as the last time he saw her, she had been bound, a kidnapped victim of my mother's crazy plan. I stood back, waiting my turn and seizing the moment to observe both my brother and his woman.

She was gorgeous and not in that American way that had become so popular. This woman was curvy and earthy and a good match for my brother. He was built like me but broader, and I could tell from his stance that he did more than *workout*. He looked like a man who was prepared for anything, a fighter, a true warrior.

His body, while not rigid, seemed in constant motion even while standing still. He was on guard, and I wondered if he had seen action at some point. Beside him, Suri was firm but soft and inviting, both in body and mannerisms. They were the epitome of the yin and yang symbol on the gym wall where I worked out.

When Suri's eyes turned to mine, I saw a world of emotions there. I'd scared her, and although I would never have hurt her, she hadn't known that last night.

"Suri," I said, reaching for her hand. "I am so very sorry, lass. I have no way to prove that my intentions were never to hurt you, but maybe with time, you will come to learn my character and see for yourself that I am truly sorry and not a threat to you."

She didn't let go of my hand and continued to gaze into my eyes. I began to feel the heat emanating from her hold on me and wondered what was going on. She continued to hold my hands and closed her eyes. When she opened them, she smiled up at me. "I accept your apology, Malcolm, and I believe that had push come to shove, you would not have hurt me."

Laughlin let out a breath, I assumed, one of relief, making me wonder what had just occurred. "Please, come inside, we have much to discuss, and lunch is ready."

I was surprised when we were led to a dining room, instead of his office, and found the others from last night present as well. I had been questioned by two of the men from the previous night, Eddy and Geoff, who were both at the dining table and wore friendly expressions.

"Sir Henry, Malcolm, these are our Canadian friends, Geoff, his son Adam, and his wife, Montana. Their friend and head of security, Eddy, his team, J2, Mike, Luke Rob, and Steve. And you may know that big ox sitting at the end, Declan Campbell."

There was a pause, then Laughlin continued. "Gentlemen, and lady," he said, nodding his head at Montana, "this is my brother, Malcolm, and his father, Henry. Now let's eat."

We took our places. I was sitting beside Laughlin and across from Suri. Henry was at the other end, next to Declan and across from Geoff.

Divide and conquer. I had to admire my brother's tactics. He would learn more through casual dining than placing either Henry or myself in the hot seat. From the other end of the table, we heard Eddy teasing Montana about passing out in the hot tub. Her eyes found Suri's, and an unspoken communication passed between the two women.

I had been watching them at the hot tub last night. That was how I was able to kidnap Suri. She'd had her hands on Montana's back, and the woman had laid down her head and fallen asleep. At least that was how it looked from my hiding spot. I glanced across the table at Suri, who was now regarding me.

She had remarkable eyes, open, with an odd assortment of colors that seemed to shift from grey to green constantly. I could tell from the way she looked at me that I was not the only one thinking about the hot tub incident. Whatever I had witnessed, I hoped I would soon learn what it was. The conversation was pretty general throughout the meal, and once the dishes were cleared away, Laughlin stood and drew Suri to her feet.

"I'm glad you are all here, as I have an announcement to make. This extraordinary woman has agreed to be my wife." A hint of color rose in Suri's cheeks at Laughlin's pronouncement. "She has made it clear that we will not have a wedding without our Canadian friends."

Grins and backslapping from the assembled guests went on for a moment.

"We are aware that you are all busy, and we are hoping you can all come back, and as such, the future Mrs. Campbell, Lady Roswell, is happy to accommodate."

"Why wait? We are here now, and there is no time like the present," Montana suggested with a glint of mischief in her eyes. "Besides, we planned on being here for a bit. What's a few more days?"

Laughlin and Suri exchanged looks. I was sure he was hoping for sooner rather than later.

"Adam and I have a beautiful chapel you may want to use for the occasion." Montana sweetened the pot. "And Declan's mother, Mrs. C, can have it readied with heather and wild-flowers in a day. Then you don't have to do anything but focus on yourself."

I gazed at my brother and soon-to-be sister-in-law. Would they bow to the pressure? I was curious to watch how Laughlin handled things. Henry had mentioned that Laughlin was formidable in both business and his personal life.

"We will take that under advisement, Montana. Thank you for your generous offer." He finished with a slight bow, ever the gentleman. "Now, if you will excuse me, I need to acquaint myself better with Malcolm."

His eyes traveled to Geoff, who was watching Laughlin almost as intensely as I was. That man was dangerous, I decided, and was glad he was one of the good guys. At least I hoped he was one of the good guys. In truth, I didn't know any of these people well enough to know.

"Geoff, perhaps you and Declan can talk a little more in-depth with Henry regarding our unsolved questions and see if we can learn any more as to the bigger plan."

"Of course, gentlemen, let's head to the meeting room." The three excused themselves and left with a carafe of coffee.

Montana and Suri regarded each other again, seeming to speak without using words. Suri kissed Laughlin on the cheek. "Montana and I will be at the lagoon if you need me."

He pulled her to him and kissed her deeply before letting her go. When he did, he told her to behave, and there was a gleam in his eyes that made me wonder what went on between the two of them in private.

Laughlin watched her walk out of the room. I think we all did, for Suri had one of the finest asses I'd ever seen. Laughlin was a lucky man. When he turned to me, his eyes shuttered. I imagine that was a force of habit he'd learned from our father, Sir Robert.

"Come, let's go somewhere we can talk." Laughlin rose,

and I followed him out of the dining room and down several connecting hallways until we sat in a garden room that over-looked the lagoon. He was keeping an eye on Suri, and I didn't blame him. If I had such a remarkable woman I was in love with, I would do the same.

"How are you feeling after all that transpired last night?" He was asking me how I felt? How very curious, as I was the bad guy.

"Honestly, I'm waiting for the other shoe to drop. I can't imagine anything positive coming of this, but I do appreciate the show of camaraderie at lunch, thank you."

Laughlin reclined in a vast antique leather chair that did nothing to dwarf his six-foot-five-inch frame. His eyes gave away nothing; he could have been thinking anything, even murdering me where I sat, and I would have no idea. "Mal-colm, let's begin again. He sat forward and reached out his hand. I sat forward and took it in my grasp. "Hello, I am Laughlin Campbell. It is very nice to meet you at long last, brother."

Chapter 2

Octavia

"**M**ove with the breath and remember that yoga without being breath-led is only an exercise. With breath, it becomes about the triad of self, energy, body, and mind." Teaching yoga had become a passion a long time ago.

Years of working in the corporate world in Australia had almost killed me.

Here, in the studio, was just a being, no stress, no attainment, no worry, only a state of being. "Where's your mind? Focus on the inside as you use a focal point with your eyes. Lean into the pose and move only when your body is in sync with your energy and your thoughts."

Years of helping others attain enlightenment were becoming burdensome. In the beginning, I took a weekend class to keep from having stress attacks. That evolved, and early 6:00 am classes before work became necessary. Soon I was hooked and couldn't get through a day without yoga.

"Forward fold and hold for a count of eight." Six months

in, I was looking for a career move. I'd made a small fortune, enough to start a rather large yoga school, after acquiring the necessary education to teach.

"Inhale as you fold up from your hips, then step or jump your legs together. Come down to the earth and into savasana." I surveyed the class of fifty participants. I still packed them in, which was the only reason I was still teaching. By all rights, I should have passed on the baton years ago. I'd been at the yoga thing almost ten years, and it was time for a sabbatical.

"Close your eyes and gaze to an internal point between your brows. Soften your facial muscles. Slow your breath and allow yourself to let go." I'd heard from Suri a few times since she left, almost three months ago. I missed her presence and our nightly wine sessions. As per her request, I put her meager items in storage and opened my condo up to Tsui, who'd come back to take over the studio for a year. It was time for this goddess to fly the coop and expand her wings.

"Relax your leg muscles, your buttocks, and hips. Relax your legs and your feet. Relax your toes. Relax your back and your belly and chest. Feel yourself sink into the earth. Imagine you are floating in a place of peace, maybe on a favorite lake or the sand at the beach. Release your tension and allow it to float away."

Suri had found the man of her dreams in Turkey, the man she had dreamt about before leaving on vacation with fellow teacher Tino. She'd confirmed for me that dreams really could come true. I'd been in love once, or thought I'd been, until I found the guy in his office with his PA.

Since then, I'd contented myself with the rare friend bene-fit, but even that hadn't been for some time. The truth was I was burnt out, giving, giving, and more giving, and lacking a way to refill myself. But that was about to change. In a few days, I would be flying to Scotland to visit Suri. From there, I didn't yet know. I wanted the freedom to go where the universe drew me, so making plans was not part of the picture.

"Move into the present space and time. Slowly open your eyes and walk in your feet. Draw your knees to your chest and rock gently from side to side. When you are ready, roll to a seated sukhasana position. Inhale your hands to the sky, and exhale to your heart's center. Namaste, and thank you for joining me today."

I bowed to the class, who returned the bow. Then enthusiastic clapping broke out. Not a usual occurrence in yoga, but I appreciated their show of enthusiasm. Tsui had been in the back. He'd been doing a great job of observing all of my master classes, as he would be taking them over.

"You have such a loyal following, Stacey. I don't know if I can do your classes justice."

"Octavia, please, Stacey is officially gone, and Octavia is getting ready for the adventure of her life and appreciates you stepping in."

"Oh, oh, she's talking about herself in the third person."

I laughed at the serious monk doing his best to be playful.

"Seriously, Tsui, my students have gotten too comfortable with my style. They need to be challenged, and I am not the one to provide it."

He nodded in understanding. "There is a message for you from Suri, and she said to call as soon as you can."

"She called the studio? That's odd."

"No, she left a message on your private machine, and I just happened to hear it when I was dropping off some things."

"That, or she wanted to say hello. Thanks, Tsui. I need to shower and have some calls to make anyway, so I'll add Suri to the list."

He nodded in affirmation and departed. I chose to stop and chat with a few senior students before heading upstairs to my loft, to clean up and make my calls. After exiting a hot shower, I threw on my casual lounge clothing, sat down with a tea and a bliss ball, and gave Suri a call.

"It's about time. I have news."

I laughed at the tone of eagerness in her voice. Patience had never been her strong suit, and she could also be a little bratty when she wanted something to happen. I summed this up to still ascending.

"Well, I'm all ears, Ms. Impatient. What's your news?"

"Laughlin and I are getting married. Can you fly out any earlier?"

I was shocked. How long had they been together, seven weeks?

"Um, yes. But are you sure this is the right move?"

"Yes. One hundred percent yes, and I need my maid-of-honor here."

I smiled at her enthusiasm. "Okay. When is the big day?"

"In three days, and I need you here before then. Laughlin can send his jet tonight if you're game, then it's only like six hours, and you can sleep on the flight over."

I wanted to protest and say it was all moving too fast. But isn't this precisely what I needed, some spontaneity to start my next chapter? I took a deep breath and let it out. I calmed my racing heart and took a few more breaths. "Okay, tonight it is, but after rush hour. How about midnight, and then I will sleep on the flight over?"

"You got it, and I will be there to pick you up. I can't wait to see you. There is so much to catch up on and, well, so many changes and shifts."

I understood that. "I'm looking forward to all of it. See you soon, my friend."

"I'll text you the details, and Octavia, I'm so happy you will be here, thank you."

"You'd better be," I huffed and then laughed. "Namaste."

"Namaste."

I hung up the phone and looked around. I'd opted not to rent out my suite while I was away. I didn't lack any money, and I preferred to keep the energy in my place clean. I needed nothing to prepare, as my newest acolyte was doing karma yoga and taking care of my plants and mail in exchange for free classes.

I hadn't purchased any fresh groceries in two weeks, slowly dwindling my fridge supply. On that note, my stomach growled. Time to seek out my dinner, then I would come back and finish packing. Like I'd taught my students, staying present is a massive part of being happy. I found that depressed people were stuck in the past. In contrast, anxious people were stuck in the future. The great Lao Tzu had said as much. I had let go of my angst of what-ifs, and breathing provided me with that ability. Now, as I looked around my apartment, I realized I was ready and very excited about seeing my friend. As I walked the two blocks to my favorite vegan restaurant, I thought about the first time I met Suri. She had been Mary back then, Mary Stanhope, and I had been Stacey.

During the first day of class introductions, participants set intentions for the week. Intentions were expressions of an approach they were dedicating themselves to during their week in New York at my studio, Everything Zen. The attendees shared why they had decided to attend the weeklong retreat, and I was struck by the repetitive theme voiced by most of the students.

All the things they wanted were valid reasons for attending a life-altering week of yoga inclusion—weight loss, gaining control of either their bodies, their minds, or both, adding more discipline. Nothing different than what I'd heard a million times before. While all those reasons were valid, there was nothing really for me to sink my teeth into until Mary spoke.

She looked directly into my eyes. "Hi. I'm Mary, and I'm here to search my soul. I'm stuck in a rut in my relationships, and I want to know why, so I can recreate myself and move on. I've got lots to be thankful for, but I know there's got to be more." She broke eye contact then. But the strength of Mary's vibrating energy had spoken to me. I knew that Mary was a natural healer. She emanated a beautiful green aura that intensified at times.

I was lost in my first impressions of Suri when I entered the restaurant and found Tsui already there. I laughed from across the room. "Great minds think alike." I plopped down on a chair opposite him.

"Did you talk to Suri? How is she?"

"Suri sounds amazing, and I have news… she is getting married and insists that I get to Scotland sooner rather than later." He nodded his head sagely. "But you already knew that, didn't you?" I said as I examined Tsui, who cracked a smile at my scrutiny.

"I had a feeling this would be our last supper for a while."

"Last supper. Biblical much?"

He laughed deeply. "Just because you grew up Baptist, Stacey, doesn't mean that everything has a biblical reference."

"Octavia, and agreed. I am assuming because you know so much, you already ordered for me?"

"Of course, now, tell me when you are leaving."

"Tonight, midnight, in a private jet no less."

"Traveling in style, Stacey. Sorry, Octavia, you must be excited."

Was I excited? "Yes, a little, I admit, but my excitement is not for my next chapter but Suri's. You know her. With all the trauma she has been through, she must be feeling very confident in this man."

Tsui nodded his head in agreement. "Suri has developed her instincts, and I think she is a good judge of character now that she has eyes to see. I'm sure whoever the guy is, he is perfect for her."

Our food arrived, and both of us were quiet as we concentrated on our meal. Tsui never spoke when he ate, as his cloistered teachings taught to be mindful of habits, including eating. I was busy going over everything in my head, assuring myself I had everything under control. We were ready to depart an hour later. "Thank you again, my friend, for taking on my business. No one else could have done it."

"You are welcome. It was time to get out of the mountains and take on a new challenge. I have led a selfless but selfish life."

"How so?" I asked. I was genuinely confused by Tsui's statement.

"In the mountainous world of Tibet, one has only to concentrate on themselves, their path to enlightenment. So in that, I have been allowed to be selfish. Our community outreach was part of our karma service, but, really, it required very little of me."

"Funny, but I never did ask how such a gorgeous Englishman became Tsui Tran."

Tsui smiled. "And now you will have to wait."

"Great, another lesson in patience, and here I thought I had fully ascended."

Tsui laughed. "No one ever truly ascends until that time arrives, Octavia. All these trappings, the classes, the meditation, and breath work are but vehicles to help connect to the divine. But in truth, the divine is all around and in us all the time."

"I'm going to miss you." I leaned in for a hug.

"Make sure you stay connected, and send pictures. Hug Suri for me, and stay safe."

"Got it." I saluted like a commander, and we parted ways. When I looked back, Tsui was already gone. I swear that man had learned more than monk ways. He was so stealthy, he reminded me more of a ninja.

Chapter 3

Malcolm

Wheezing like an older man, I flopped down onto the lounger and watched as Declan picked up where I left off, sparring with Laughlin. I was welcomed into the family fold with no questions asked. My stupid act, forgiven if not forgotten, and this newfound connection to my brother, his fiancée, and friends was a bona fide gift.

We were currently sparring, and although I owned a host of gyms across Europe and worked out regularly, I had never done much cardio and had never fought. Laughlin, raised by order of Templar Knights, had been sparring since the age of six and was both fierce and deadly.

Suri and Montana were also sparring and were quite a sight to behold. Eddy stood by, closely observing Suri's moves and correcting where need be, as per Laughlin's request. After all that had happened to her in such a short period of time, Laughlin wanted Suri to at least have the basic rudiments of self-defense to draw from. Suri was a strong, flexible woman, but Montana was putting Suri through her paces.

"They are well-matched," I observed to no one in particular.

"That they are. I never did get to see Sir Robert and Laughlin sparring, but I heard about it. Laughlin is deadly." Henry watched, his eyes rounding at a particularly hard jab that Declan delivered to my brother. I had been watching and referring to the ladies, but Henry had been watching the men.

"Declan has been training since he was a young boy but not in an official capacity, like inheriting a Templar throne. Funny, considering he is as deeply immersed in Templar history as the rest of us," Geoff commented as he watched the two men with eyes I doubted missed much. He was sharp and reminded me of a bird of prey.

"How so?" Marcus asked.

"We have lots to catch you up on, Sir Marcus, but to summarize, Declan Campbell, Suri Sinclair, and Montana Stanford (McGregor) have a very distant relation in common from Scotland. Maybe when the wedding is complete, we should sit down. As you are Laughlin's second, you should be aware of all that is happening within the Masons."

I wasn't listening to whatever they said next because Suri and Montana's sparring was ramping up a notch and had grabbed my attention. I noticed the yard's activity slowed and then stopped as everyone's eyes were on the two women.

They were of equal height, but other than a sprinkling of freckles across their noses and cheeks, they shared no resemblance. Montana was reasonably thin and in excellent shape, with not an ounce of fat on her body except in the right places. Her husband's eyes followed her as she moved around like a dangerous cat.

Suri was Marilyn Monroe reborn, voluptuous, with long, lean muscles and a perfect ass. My brother was a lucky man, and I hoped to find such a remarkable woman one day. Having Suri as a prisoner for several hours gave me insight into her character, and I found myself impressed with her. It was because of me that she was now learning to defend herself. Not that it would have helped her when I got a hold of her, as I'd put a chloroform cloth over her mouth and nose, knocking her out in seconds. My newly found half-brother, Laughlin, had forgiven me, the onus of the blame placed on our mutual father, Sir Robert, and my mentally unstable mother.

Suri was down on her back now, Montana kneeling over her, the victor. I glanced to Laughlin, whose mouth was set in a grim line. Laughlin kept quiet, but I could tell it bothered him seeing his woman tossed to the ground.

He must have felt me looking at him, for he glanced my way. "I'm ready for a swim and some lunch. How about you?" He was looking at me but addressing everyone present.

"Aye, a swim sounds perfect. Gentlemen," I said, acknowledging my sideline mates, "I will see you at lunch."

I followed Laughlin into the lagoon, relishing the gentle liquid heat that loosened my weary muscles. Montana and Suri headed for the hot tub. I wondered if they did this to give us space.

"You did well today for a gym jock."

I was pulled from my thoughts and laughed at his title for me. "Thanks, bro. I've been thinking all morning that I should be offering self-defence classes in my gyms. I have come to realize that machines can only get you so far. You need interaction and motion to help build other elements of the body."

"Suri would agree with you. I have watched her doing yoga and have to say that nothing I have done has provided me with the nimbleness that she displays."

I floated on my back, thinking about yoga. I knew very little about the discipline but decided I would learn. "I would like to know more. I'm not sure I would like to do yoga but seeing its benefits would undoubtedly give me more insight. Gyms need to offer more variety, and I am more than happy to be the catalyst for change."

"Spoken like a true visionary. Stay around a bit, and you will see its benefits. Also, I have my jet picking up Suri's best friend in New York. She owns a very successful yoga business called Everything Zen, Healing and Yoga Inc. Maybe she can help fill you in on the business side of things."

"Sounds intriguing. Is this friend single?"

Laughlin laughed and then realized I was serious. "You're a good-looking guy, Malcolm, how come you're single?"

"I've had my share, but nothing fulfilling. I seem to draw the wrong kind of woman. Like your friend Marcus, I've had a parade of gym women, as I like to call them. They are very different from your yoga woman. Not to put all women in a box, but I find many women who frequent the gym have low self-esteem and tend to compensate by working their bodies to create something *perfect*. Suri is very different from anyone I usually come into contact with at the gym. She is calm and confidant in herself and her looks. How did you two meet?"

"Quite by accident. Well, I think by accident, but we are still looking into that."

"What do you mean? Either it is an accident, or it isn't."

My brother's cloak and dagger explanation seemed ridiculous. "I was in Turkey on Mason business with the other master Masons. I was getting ready to leave our meeting, the last one out the door because I was also there, unknown to anyone else, to investigate my father's death. I was just walking out of the men's bathroom in the bar where we'd held our meeting when Suri came peeling around the corner and slammed into me. She mumbled about shooters and needing help. I waited for the men chasing her to pass the bar as I steered her out into the alley. Then she passed out, and I carried her home."

"How very romantic of you. So, what's the mystery? It sounds like an accident to me."

"Suri is a Sinclair; her ex-husband was in line to take her father's position as lead Mason for the eastern United States. The gunmen were attempting to assassinate a Templar who had infiltrated the SOG as a spy for us. Do you think that is a coincidence? In addition to that, the guy friend she traveled with has disappeared."

Even though Templar conspiracy tactics were unknown to me, I was not one to question things a great deal, but what he'd just shared gave me pause. Laughlin's story was intriguing, and I had to agree there was more going on than mere coincidence. "How do the Canadian people fit into this story?"

"Geoff contacted me after he got wind of my father's death. We had both realized that someone high up was erecting barriers through essential communication channels, somewhere in our order."

"And Declan?"

"Declan's best friend and mentor went to Cambridge on a mission for the Masons and disappeared. Declan's great ancestor and Montana's great ancestor were half-sisters. Geoff has informed me that the death of both her parents is also not as it appears. There is a mystery afoot that involves us all, and I think your mother, Annie, knows more than she is letting on."

I was about to answer when the lagoon filled up with the rest of the crew, except Geoff and Henry, who could be seen on the patio drinking and chatting like old friends. I wasn't a sentimental person usually, but it warmed my heart to see that Henry, my father, was accepted into Laughlin's fold with me.

Laughlin lifted Suri in his arms, and she wrapped her long, sexy legs around his waist. He leaned down and claimed her mouth with a deep, enviable kiss. For the first time in a while, I was jealous of someone else. I could go right now and pick up a woman if I wanted to, but it would just be sex, and I was tired of the whole game. I wanted something more meaningful. I desired a hot, sexy, smart woman in my arms who would let me take the lead.

My thirtieth birthday was around the corner, so maybe this year would be my year and I would get lucky. Laughlin released Suri's mouth, and her eyes opened and gazed into his. I felt like an interloper and turned to leave.

"Malcolm, my girlfriend Octavia is flying in early tomorrow. Do you think you could do me a huge favor and pick her up from the private hangar at Edinburgh airport?"

I felt it an off request, but of course, I said yes.

"Wonderful. I think Octavia would like to meet you as you own a large gym franchise and she has a hugely successful yoga company. I'm sure you two will have plenty to talk about." Suri's eyes glittered with mischief.

Laughlin's eyes narrowed as he regarded Suri, but he said nothing.

Adam came sloshing over then, with Montana on his back. "So, have you made a decision yet? Are we heading to the Highlands gateway, to old Castle Campbell?"

Suri looked at Laughlin, for what—permission? His opinion? For him to take control? Montana had offered the castle yesterday morning, and now the couple needed to make a decision.

"We would be honored to be your guests," Laughlin finally answered.

Montana bounced up and down on Adam's back in excitement. He grinned but said nothing, probably enjoying the fabulous friction her nether region was creating on his hips. Damn, at this rate, I would have to go home and pump one out.

"Who else is coming? Are your parents flying in from Boston?"

Suri shook her head in resignation. "No, but my sister is due to fly in tonight, and my girlfriend from school lives in Glasgow. I already spoke to her, and she will be taking the train, as it is about two hours travel for her. Octavia is on her way, and I would love for Tsui to come, but he is watching Octavia's business for her."

"That's a small list," Montana said as she slid down from Adam's back. "I have things to do, gotta go. See you all later." Montana left the pool and disappeared into the house.

"She will be calling Mrs. C to make sure the chapel and the guest rooms are ready. No doubt she'll have the town picking thousands of wildflowers and employing them all to put on your small event."

Suri frowned. "I don't want to put anyone out. The wedding is a small affair, as I wanted it to be."

Adam smiled indulgently. "We have worked hard to revitalize the community. We finally have a thriving town after years of education and building. So trust me when I say that by coming to our castle, you are giving work to the town and contributing to its independence."

"Really?" Laughlin looked intrigued. "I am very interested in your philanthropic works, Adam. You will have to tour me so I can see all these good works."

"I would be honored, Laughlin. The town has come a long way since we first toured it, years ago. There were no jobs, no trades left, so the kids were moving away. All that was left was the retired community, and they couldn't get the help they needed, either. By revitalizing the community, we created education and trade jobs. Everything required is now offered, including my little gem, an art school. It was Montana's vision. I just do what I always do and support her in making it happen."

Suri's eyes lit up. The woman was motivated by what Adam had shared. Her gaze shifted to me. "Maybe we could add a gym and yoga studio, a satellite size for the locals, and start a kids' program. What do you think, Malcolm?"

I had never been part of building anything but my empire. From talking to Laughlin, I knew that the environment was a huge issue, and he was working diligently to make a difference here and abroad. This could be my way of paying back for my recent wrong actions, a way to connect in a more meaningful way. "I think it's a lovely idea, as long as we're not stepping on anyone's toes, and if it's needed." My gaze shifted to Adam.

He was observing me intently, with eyes I could swear saw my soul. "We like to draw our family and friends into our endeavors, Malcolm." He smiled then, and it reached his eyes.

For me, that was the green light needed for allowing Laughlin's new friends to be mine as well. "Then I am happy to offer anything I have. Maybe you and Laughlin can create a blueprint that other townships could adopt. There are many small towns here in Scotland that could use the help—"

"What about tourism, Adam?" Suri interrupted. "Have you thought about offering the outdoor Highland experience? Add in some weapons classes for us Americans."

"We have talked about it. As Declan is a weapons master, he may be willing to take it on. We've been keeping him so busy in Canada that he hasn't had a chance to do anything here in Scotland."

Just then, Declan's eyes turned our way. "You'd better not be talking about me if ye want to live another day," he declared, giving us the gimlet eye.

"Don't get your panties in a knot, you giant Scot. Yer going home tomorrow; we're hosting the wedding," Adam called.

The Highlander grinned. "Och, yer in for a treat, me ma

is the best cook, aye?" We all broke out in peals of laughter at the use of his thick brogue.

"I should be getting along, as it sounds like tomorrow will be a long day. And mine begins with the airport. Should I bring Octavia here or meet you at the castle?"

"We can travel together. Henry is going ahead at first light with the rest, I'm told. Unless you'd rather drop her off and meet us?" Laughlin's eyes glittered with amusement. I would prefer to go with the lass alone if she was anything like Suri, but I wasn't going to say that out loud.

"Marcus and Lenore, Suri's sister, will be traveling with us as well." Laughlin was trying to hold back his laughter now. So this was how it was going to go… Suri was hooking her friend with me and her sister, Lenore, with Laughlin's best mate. I felt like I was a lad in school and wondered at her antics.

"Fine," I conceded. "I'll bring Octavia here, but breakfast had better be ready." Now Laughlin did laugh, and I wasn't offended in the least that it was at my expense. "My lady," I said, kissing Suri's hand and exiting the lagoon. I could feel Laughlin's eyes boring into my back, and it was my turn to laugh at his expense. It was evident, he didn't like anyone touching his woman; so possessive, that one.

Chapter 4

Octavia

The ride across the Atlantic had been relaxing. Once I boarded, I was offered a late-night snack and a beverage of my choice and was happy that they had a wide variety of herbal teas to choose from. The chairs were large and luxurious, and I melted into my seat and contemplated life.

Would Suri be somewhat changed? How wonderful could her new beau be? I knew Suri would have loved to have Tsui here as well, but he'd already committed to the school. I felt selfish in that I could have had others fill in for a week for him while he was here.

It suddenly hit me that the school, despite my protestations otherwise, was a source of angst for me. I was worried about an inanimate object. I laughed outright at how I had missed such a simple epiphany.

I grabbed my phone and texted Suri.

Me: *I feel like a selfish oaf. If you're awake and still want Tsui at the wedding, go ahead and bring him. I just realized that he could be there for you. I'm sorry for being so selfish.*

Suri: *Lol, I am still awake and just showed your message to Laughlin. He's rolling his eyes at you. I will call Tsui in the morning and see if he wants to come. Be safe and see you in a few hours.*

I put my phone away and let my chair down into a bed, then I placed my earphones on and listened to the alpha wave music for induced sleep. I awoke a few hours later, to find a carafe of freshly pressed coffee and lemon water waiting for me as per my pre-flight instructions. Suri had mentioned we'd be breaking our fast together, so I'd made sure to not order breakfast.

I opened the shade and saw that the sun was cresting the horizon, a sight I hadn't seen since living in Australia. It was breathtaking, and the warmth it created inside me sparked a wave of gratefulness—to be alive, to be free, to be on this adventure of a lifetime.

The plane touched down, and I removed my seatbelt. Walking down the stairs, I looked for Suri. There was only one person on the tarmac, and he was a gorgeous man. Super tall and muscular but lean, his hair had a windblown look, and he appeared as if he'd walked off the cover of a magazine.

I felt the heat rise in all the right places. Even from a distance, this man did all kinds of things to me. I wondered who he was and why he was here. Maybe I could get his phone number and have some fun before leaving Scotland.

He stalked over to me, and I found myself holding my breath. As he got closer, I could see his eyes and admired the unusual color as well as the freshly shaven chiseled jaw. But what caught my interest the most was the sexual energy emanating from him in waves.

I felt my knees weaken and heat move down into my core. I hadn't felt this kind of attraction in years and wondered why now and why so suddenly?

"Hello, Octavia," the giant of a man said, reaching out his hand to take mine. I tentatively reached out one of mine, which he took, placing a gentle kiss on the back. "I am Malcolm, Laughlin's brother, and I'm here to pick you up." He grinned then at the double meaning in *pick you up.*

He looked so roguish when he said it that I couldn't help but laugh. He was genuinely a delight. "Well, I am happy to be picked up," I said with a naughty twinkle in my eye. Teasing this veritable giant would be fun.

"Now, now, Miss Octavia, don't tease unless you mean to make good on your promises." His voice dropped and deepened as he spoke, sending delicious shivers down my spine. He moved closer and peered deeply into my eyes.

I felt my breath catch the moment I became aware that this man knew the effect he had on me. I felt upended and set afloat, which made perfect sense as I was swimming with the sharks. He reached out and gently gripped my chin. Then he placed a soft kiss on my lips.

When he pulled back, his eyes had darkened, and his pupils were dilated. He was as turned on as I was, and I hoped he'd make good on it later when the chance presented itself. We were interrupted by my luggage being deposited at my feet, one enormous backpack that held almost all of my clothing. Being a minimalist had its advantages.

Malcolm grinned and picked up my backpack. "Let's go, lass, breakfast is waiting."

Oh, his gentle accent was a living thing that had a constant run of shivers moving down my spine. There was another name for this, I knew—Kundalini—when one's energy awakened and moved through the chakras. Malcolm woke me up inside. There was no other way of describing it.

The ride to Roswell Castle was a blend of heightened awareness, because of the man next to me, and blissful sights. My eyes were moving from the wonders outside my window to the hunk of a man beside me. I loved watching the muscles in his thigh flex as he moved his foot on the pedals. The corded muscles on his forearms seemed like living things as his hands moved on the steering wheel. Turned on and happy, I wanted to laugh out loud and couldn't wait to confide all of my feelings to Suri.

We arrived at a gate and took the long driveway up to the medieval castle. Standing outside, were Suri and Laughlin, and she looked golden in the light of the sun. Her energy sparkled and moved around her in a dance. She was happy was my first thought. Tears sprang to my eyes at seeing her so alive.

As soon as Malcolm parked the car, I jumped out and raced over to her. We crashed in our enthusiasm to greet each other. Now my tears leaked down my cheeks, and when I pulled back, I saw that hers did too. "Suri, it feels like years since I last saw you, not a few months."

She grinned now, wiping the tears from her cheeks. "I know, and I have missed you so much. Thank you for being here with me. Octavia, this is my love, Laughlin." His resemblance to Malcolm struck me, but their energies were entirely different. Before me, the man carried a weight on his shoulders and exuded an old soul intelligence, with a masterful command. He was a leader and no doubt was the leader in all of his dealings and relationships.

"Laughlin, it is very nice to meet the perfect man for Suri, at long last."

His shuttered eyes gave nothing away but offered me a slight bow of the head as he said, "It is entirely my pleasure," and kissed the back of my hand. These lordly Scotsmen were so polite, compared to the New Yorkers whom I'd been engaging in casual hook-ups with these last years.

"Come inside. My sister and Laughlin's best mate, Marcus,

are here and waiting for us. Then I will give you the tour before we leave."

"Leave?"

"Didn't Malcolm tell you? Oh, I have so much to tell you." Suri gave Malcolm the eye before hooking her arm through mine.

The men followed behind, with Malcolm carrying my backpack. Suri led us through a series of spacious hallways containing a rich tapestry of furniture and art ranging over different periods in history. This castle cried out that the owner had exquisite taste.

The breakfast room was sunny, and the side table was laden with an extensive buffet, enough to feed twenty people. "Marcus, Lenore, this is Octavia, my bestie from the Big Apple." A young, refined-looking man with dark blond hair and remarkable eyes stood and bowed over my hand. "A plea-sure to meet the best friend of the lovely Suri. Welcome to Scotland, Octavia."

These men put the Australian and American men at a disadvantage. Maybe it was their wealth. Admittedly, I had worked in the upper echelons of the tech industry in Brisbane and Sidney but had never dated anyone. Perhaps they could give these lordly Scots a run for their money?

Beside him, a petite version of Suri stood up. She had a diminutive stature, and her energy seemed polite and curious. She was younger than Suri, and she appeared sheltered. Being the younger sister, I assumed this was accurate. Her smile was wide and open, with the most adorable dimple in the corners of her rosy cheeks that highlighted her sensual mouth.

Marcus couldn't keep his eyes off her, and I was sure she would fall for him, although right now, she seemed aware of his attentions and paid them no mind. *Good for her,* I thought, *keeping the guy on his toes.*

With the introductions over, I was about to sit when

Malcolm gently took hold of my arm and steered me over to the buffet. "Let me assist, as there are some dishes set out that you may be unfamiliar with. They are traditional Scottish fare."

The heat emanating from his hand was having an impact on me. The man was like a walking sex god, and for the first time in forever, I wanted to sample someone's goods.

"Be aware that we have a lot of meat at breakfast. Do you eat meat?"

"I do. I prefer not to eat pork or beef and stay more to the lighter white meats because of digestion, more than anything. However, ultimately, I prefer vegetable-based proteins. But I am a foodie and will eat whatever is available."

A gentle blush appeared on Malcolm's face, my comment no doubt making him think of his cock. I glanced down at his package, indicating that I had meant what I said. He coughed politely and then continued.

"This is black pudding, although very popular here and in Great Britain, I don't recommend it, based on your prefer- ences. We have baked beans, which may be preferable, as well as a vegetable medley, tatties, and scones, and three different types of eggs, potato patties, and muesli and fruit. That last bit is Suri's influence."

Malcolm was standing close enough that I could smell his aftershave and, beneath that, his subtle odor, spicy with a hint of sandalwood and citrus. I took a deep breath and allowed the smells of him and the feast to wash over me.

"I do love a variety," I said, amusement pulling the corner of my mouth into a hint of a smile. Still gazing intently at the yummy man before me, I licked my lips.

Malcolm's eyes slightly narrowed. "I can see you enjoy being playful, with a hint of brattiness. Keep that up, Miss Octavia, and see where it lands you." Then Malcolm moved down to the coffee carafes and poured himself a mug while I stood gaping.

Suri sidled up beside me then. "You may want to close your maw, Octavia. You look like a fish." I slammed my mouth shut to a peal of tinkling giggles beside me. "Whatever does Malcolm mean by *surprised where it lands me*? I'm assuming he means in the sack?"

"One can only hope. If he gives as good as Laughlin, then I can tell you from first-hand experience, it is well worth seeing where it lands you."

I gazed at Suri in shock. "Why, you've become a little hoyden." I was blushing and laughing at her look of surprise. "Gotcha," I exclaimed."

"Oh my goodness, I've missed you, O. I'm so glad you could accommodate leaving New York a few days early."

"Let's get some food, and you can catch me up on what's been going on." Just then, more tinkling laughter, this time from Lenore, who was still seated beside Marcus. "She seems to be enjoying herself. Is this the first time those two have met?"

Suri's brows narrowed in concern. "It is, and I hope to intercede. Marc likes women for a short time, not a long time, and doesn't usually go for women like Lenore. Sure, she is the right age, but Marcus likes those fake Barbie doll girls, and as you can see, Lenore is a petite beauty and nothing like the runway models you'd see back in New York."

Suri led me away from the table, Malcolm's eyes never leaving me. Once we were safely nestled in a private area with no one else, I took a deep breath and slowly let it out. "That brother-in-law of yours is so hot. When I got off the plane, his energy hit me like a wave. I have never felt such intense sexual connection with anyone before."

"I'm still getting to know him."

"He is so delicious, Suri. I think I need to tap that. Does that sound terrible?"

Suri giggled. "Not in the least, but I will give you fair warning. Malcolm is looking for *the one*. He wants a woman in his life full time, and if you sleep with him, he will undoubtedly look at you as a woman who is interested in the same. Once you do succumb, it is futile to resist, as the Campbell brothers usually get their way."

The idea of having amazing sex was one thing, but being with a man ongoing? I'd never considered it, and I was beginning to see it was because I had never made room for it. Riding that thought was my surprise at missing something so obvious. My quest for the next was already proving fruitful, as maybe Malcolm was my next.

"The better question is you and Laughlin. How did this all come about?"

Suri lounged back. "It all began with a run-in in Turkey. But before that, I had been in meditation and examining what happened with Tino."

"He never made it back, by the way. He never came back to the studio. Do you know what happened to him?"

Suri shook her head. "No idea, but Laughlin is looking into his disappearance. We don't think his invite to Turkey was just a nice friend vacay. I was on the beach because he'd pushed for us to have sex, and as you know, I have zero attraction to Tino. Nice guy and a great instructor but not my type. He'd assumed by traveling together that he would be getting some action. When I vehemently declined, he kicked me out, and I ended up in a B&B. Then that night, I witnessed a crime and, running blindly, hit the wall when Laughlin and I collided. Everything seemed disconnected and non-coincidental until we started putting the pieces together. He told me he would keep me safe, and that also meant from myself. I had no idea, O, that I was such a brat until I met him. I have fallen hard, and I know he has too. I am his first love, and despite having been married, you know that Edward was no great love of mine. I was bullied into the marriage just like I was bullied in my job. But it's all in the past, and I am far from being bullied now."

"So, you have discovered your bratty side. What does that mean for you? After all, your new life has been about transcendence and transmutation. How does this fit in?"

Suri sat forward, her eyes glittering with excitement. "You know how in yoga, we are taught to become friends with our darker nature? Yet, we still reach for the light. Like the lotus flower, our roots are buried in the murk and mud, yet our flowers, our enlightened selves, exist above water and show only our best versions of ourselves? I thought that was me when I left the Big Apple. But being in a different environment, I realized I was not that person. Or rather that my roots were as important as my divine development. I could see clearly from both ends for the first time, and now, I'm not afraid to just be me. Laughlin brings that out, my character, and holds it close to his heart. He makes me whole, gathering all of my pieces into one place."

Suri took my hands in hers. "The rest is still a mystery, a Templars' mystery that we are figuring out, and that is all I can say for now regarding that."

"Wow, I think that is the most romantic story I have ever heard. You should say that as part of your vows."

"I intend to. That's the first time I've verbalized Laughlin and me and what he does for me, so thank you, O, for asking the question."

"You're welcome. Now tell me, where are we traveling to today?"

"Oh, we are going to another castle, owned by friends of ours. You're going to love them, O. Montana is so much fun, and Adam, her husband, is quite a man. They have a beautiful chapel that is being decorated for our use tomorrow."

"What about a dress? Have you thought about that? Everything seems so rush, rush, why?"

"In answer to question one, I have a seamstress appointment when we arrive, and the dress will be ready on time. In answer to question two, our Canadian friends have to go back soon, and instead of waiting, we decided to have our ceremony sooner rather than later, while those closest to us are here. Laughlin's peerage would require him to have a large society wedding, and you know my feelings about that. Whisking ourselves away out of necessity removes that issue. Adam is a photographer, well, an artist and quite famous, and she is—"

"Hold the phone! Are you talking about Adam and Montana Northrop? She is the drummer from *Behind Blue Eyes*, and he is a world-famous artist whose work is in every country in the world?"

Suri seemed taken aback. "You know them?"

"Of course, I know them. Everyone does, as the two are a huge, worldwide success. I can't believe you don't know that."

Suri looked seriously alarmed, and I couldn't help but laugh. "Here, I have her band in my Spotify list, take a listen." Scrolling through my list, I found several songs by the band, *Behind Blue Eyes*. I quickly found a ballad that showcased their voices beautifully and hit play.

When the song ended, Suri looked spellbound. "Wow, I had no idea. Thanks for sharing with me, O." Just then, the brothers entered the room, and seeing them side by side gave me a new appreciation for Scottish men. Both were tall and fit. Laughlin looked the more dangerous of the two, while Malcolm's vibe was sexually charged. A vision of him taking me right there on the lounger played before my eyes before I blinked it away.

"Laughlin," Suri stood up and jumped into his arms, "O just played me a song by Montana's band, and it was so amazing. Do you think she would sing our wedding song?"

He smiled down at her, completely smitten. "I'm sure she wouldn't mind, love. You are her new friend, after all, and she loves the spotlight."

"O? I like it, kind of like 'The Story of O'. Did you see the movie, O? It was quite the adventure into BDSM." Malcolm spoke like Suri hadn't just been talking about her wedding and we were the only two in the room. He continued, gazing at me with an intensity that made me shiver. "The power exchange was divine," Malcolm continued, "although I didn't like how the story played out, with the woman being reduced and losing all of her power. But then again, she found that, in being nothing, she had everything. Almost sounds like a yoga story, eh, O?"

Oh dear lord, his words and tone were sending me over the edge. With great effort, I pulled my gaze from his, to find that Laughlin and Suri had disappeared, which was probably for the best because I needed to make a stand. Now was the time before our flirtations got out of control.

"Malcolm, while your sultry voice and bad boy words make me horny as hell, I don't know what I want beyond you in my bed for the best sex of your life and, hopefully, mine. Beyond that, I am not offering anything, and I don't want any weirdness, either. I'm here for Suri and her big day, okay, big guy?"

I was standing toe to toe with him now, glaring up into his eyes with strength and intention. I found it easy to cow people in business by being abrupt. He regarded me like I was a tiny bug that had landed on his arm, and it infuriated me. "Do you hear me, you giant ox, I—"

Malcolm scooped me up and threw me over his shoulder.

"Put me down this instant," I commanded, kicking my legs.

He ignored me until we reached the staircase, where everyone else was standing and chatting about our departure time for the trip to the Highlands.

"Put me down you, you—"

Smacks rang out as Malcolm's hand landed sharply on my ass a few times.

"You didn't just spank me!" I shrieked. "Just wait until you put me down. I know karate, and I will make you pay for that."

"I'm hoping so, lass." Malcolm sounded amused. "Excuse us, O and I have some things to discuss before we leave."

"Ooo, don't you just wish," I said, kicking and pummelling his back with my fists. "Suri, get this giant arse to put me down this minute."

Suri looked as if she would intercede when Laughlin placed a hand on her shoulder and pulled her to him. Instead, she shrugged and said, "Maybe you should hear what he has to say, Octavia."

I was about to answer when a loud smack landed on my backside as Malcolm stomped up the stairs. As we got to the top and turned the corner, peals of laughter from down below followed us.

Chapter 5

Malcolm

When the blonde spitfire stood toe to toe with me, my cock sprang to life with the challenge. Octavia didn't give a damn about what I thought, nor did she seem particularly in need of catching me. She was genuine and alive, and I wanted her desperately. Our battle lines were drawn. It was time to deliver, or she would lose respect for me, and the idea of *we* would be short-lived.

I pushed open the door to her guest room with my foot and then kicked it shut. Moving to the bed and perching on its edge, I transitioned O from my shoulder to my lap in a nanosecond. Wrapping one of my legs over hers, I tipped her down until her face hovered just above the carpeted floor.

"Now, listen up, you aggressive little sprite. I say when, and I say how. You get to concede or say no. I want you badly, but I will not spoil our experience by being a one-night stand. You have all the power, O, so what will it be? A spanking for your attitude and part as friends? Or, a spanking and the best sex of your life?" I waited, giving her a moment to sort through her feelings and give me a straight answer. "You have three seconds to answer me, Tinkerbell."

"Go to hell, Malcolm. I don't have to answer you."

"You're right," I said, landing a hard spank on her perfect bubble ass, "but I think you will." I landed a dozen hard spanks on her backside. She screeched like I was killing her, but I knew that through her jeans, the pain was minimal. Her shrieking was from her defiance. I pulled her jeans down in one quick motion and continued my assault on her pink backside, which quickly turned to bright red under my ministrations. The more I spanked, the quieter she got until all was quiet except for the occasional grunt from her perfect mouth.

I stopped spanking but kept her draped over my lap, gently squeezing her hot backside and holding it in my grip as I spoke. "Now that I have your attention, I will ask again. Would you like to have some fun with me, O? I believe you when you said we could have amazing sex, but if what I just did has changed your mind, then I will let you go, no hard feelings. But if you want me, you'd better say it. Consider this your first lesson in power exchange, O. You must say what you want, and I will not accept anything else."

"Yes."

"Yes, what, O?"

"Yes, I would like to have sex with you, and I'm open to more. I don't know what, exactly, but right now, I need you."

That was all I needed to hear. We could figure out the rest later. I ran a finger down her soaked slit. I was both shocked and incredibly turned on that she was soaking for me. The spanking was foreplay for this luscious woman. Beneath me, O ground her hips into my thigh as I ran my finger up and down her moist crease. She was hot and ready, but I wanted to draw this out.

I removed my leg, and she widened hers in response, so receptive. I pressed down on her hard little bud, and she moaned loudly, bucking her hips. My cock was already hard, but her moans and squeals were sending shockwaves through me. My trousers became a painful prison for my growing manhood.

I lifted her off my lap and placed her on the bed on her knees. Then I pressed her back down until her chest lowered on the bed and her bouncy ass was nice and high. Undoing my trousers, I plunged into her waiting entrance. O squealed with immediate release. Her channel was squeezing and milking my cock so intensely that I was almost afraid she'd break me. Her molten lava walls embraced me, inviting me in. I slowed down my strokes and angled deeper. The vixen let out a little growl and then mewled like a kitten as I took her deep.

"Oh. My. God. Don't stop!"

She was close to losing herself, and I wanted to watch her face as she came undone. I pulled out and turned her onto her back, placing her knees over my shoulders. Octavia's eyes were glassy, her gorgeous lips parted, as she gazed up at me with her dilated, trusting eyes. I felt a pull, not in my cock, which now plunged back inside her welcoming channel. This pull, I felt in my heart. O was a woman I could fall hard for, and I almost stopped pumping into her with the wonderment of it all. I wanted her, all of her.

"Say my name, Octavia. Say it, and when you orgasm, I want you to scream it." Her lips curled into a slight bow. "Yes, sir, Malcolm." Oh, she knew how to play me, and at that moment, I was reminded who of the two of us was in control, and it wasn't me. I reached down and began thumbing her pert nipples, drawing them into sharpened peaks. Her eyes, while on me, had gone down to mere slits as she processed the sensations I was delivering.

"Please, don't stop. I'm so close... Malcolm!" She fell apart, and as she did, I hammered into her, chasing my release and riding the wave, and as I did, she crested and fell again. We were both breathing heavily as I stayed suspended over her until my raging hard-on receded from its release.

Then I dropped down on the bed and pulled her to me. Both of us were silent as our heart rates dropped and our breathing returned to normal. I wondered what she was thinking about when she broke her silence with, "That was the best sex I've had in forever, but I will be honest with you. It can't go any further than this."

I would play her game. "Fine with me, O." Beside me, she stiffened. If she thought I would beg, she had it backward. But I could play the long game, and now that I knew her head and her body were at complete odds with each other, waiting would be easy.

Laughlin wasn't the only one with a game face. I could be blank and inscrutable, like him and my birth father. As Octavia peered up at me, I could see her searching for answers, but I'd already given her one by acting the caveman. Now it was up to her.

"Well, uh, that's good then. We can be friends, uh, with benefits."

"I'm sorry, what are you talking about, friends with bene- fits? Is this an American thing?"

She laughed, and I liked the way her soul seemed to bubble along with her laughter. "It is an American thing. Made popular by a movie that came out about ten years ago."

"Well then, lass, you should find an American who is happy to be your friend with added benefits. But that is not me. I'm sorry." I stood and started to get dressed. "No doubt we will be leaving soon, and you should get dressed. Thank you, Octavia, for a wonderful time, and you know where I am if you change your mind."

She didn't say a word, just watched me dress. I uttered one more goodbye before I gently shut the door behind me.

Descending the stairs, I found Laughlin, who seemed like he'd been waiting for me.

"Well done, brother, I didn't know you were that type of man."

"We haven't got to that part of the bonding yet, Loc."

He bellowed out sharp laughter, and I joined. "Good point. So how did it go?"

"She wants a friend with benefits. Damn Aussie."

Laughlin laughed again. "I did the same to Suri, within a few hours of meeting her. I wouldn't allow her to defy me, and I thought it was good to let her know from the beginning what type of man I was. Then she could process and decide for herself if I was what she wanted."

"You did what, exactly?"

"Tanned her behind."

"Really? I can't imagine the need to draw that line so quickly, as she is such a perfect woman. When she was tied in my basement, I threatened to keep her for myself."

As expected, my brother growled at me in warning, his eyes going black.

"I meant no disrespect, and I'm glad things worked out for you two."

He calmed down and steered me to his den and a glass of scotch. It wasn't even noon yet, but he had the best scotch money could buy, so I wouldn't turn down a shot.

"On day three, Suri approached me about our relation-ship. She was due to fly home and wanted to know where we stood. I pulled an Octavia move and told her I couldn't commit to more than what we were doing, for two reasons. I wasn't convinced that she wasn't part of the Templar plan from the beginning, and two, I'd had a bad experience in my past and didn't know if I was capable of a relationship. Even now, I'm constantly learning. Suri makes it easy until she doesn't, and then things get interesting."

"Oh? How so?" I was curious as to how Suri could upend someone as strong and stalwart as Laughlin.

"Well, about a week into our relationship. Suri promised me she would stay indoors while I attended a meeting. When I came back, I found her exiting the ocean, naked. I was about to call out to her and saw two men in the shadows, stalking her. I shot one, and the other got away. When I was done chasing down the second guy who got away, I came back to find her doing reiki on the guy I'd shot, in an attempt to save his life."

"Get out, she didn't?"

"Oh yes, she did, and when I asked her about it, she told me she shared her light with anyone in need or some such crap. I lost my shit. Needless to say, she had her first discipline trip over my lap, and she has been a good girl ever since."

"Indeed, well, good for you."

Laughlin's brow creased as he thought. "The thing of it is I knew if I didn't get the message across, she would be continually putting her life in danger, and as much as I love being her knight in shining armor, as my affection for her grew, I was genuinely concerned for her well-being."

"That is understandable," I replied.

"You have a strategy for Octavia then?"

"Yes, and she will crawl to me when she is ready. I have told her, no friends with benefits for this man. I showed her what she could expect from me, and now she will know what she is missing. But believe me, brother, she will come crawling to me and beg me for more. Then I get to make the choices, and I have the power."

He downed his scotch. "As long as the lass doesn't get hurt, Malcolm. Suri will have my balls if you mistreat her best friend."

"I understand, and I promise, whatever happens, it will be Octavia's choosing, and I will honor and respect her decision."

"Good, now that is settled. I must check in on Marcus. He is all over Suri's sister, and his record is worse than mine."

"Really? Marc just seems like a guy who loves life and likes to have fun."

"Oh, he is that for sure," Laughlin responded, "but he uses them for six weeks and then dumps them. Suri will kill him if he messes around with her sister and then dumps her. Suri bonded with Sophie, Marc's last girlfriend. She helped her overcome some issues, the result of which removed the need for surgery. Sophie loves Suri and would be at our wedding if Marc wasn't coming."

I laughed at the very idea. "Poor you, it seems your Suri makes friends very easily."

"Aye, she is very approachable. Speaking of, she and Lenore are in the lagoon. I'd better get them out, as they need to get ready to leave."

"Do what you need to, Laughlin. I'm ready and will pass on the message to them."

"Thank you. I have some last-minute arrangements to see to. See you at the car in an hour." He dismissed me then, and I slipped out of his space and headed to the back patio. I found the girls in the lagoon, lying on mats and giggling about something. Marc sat in the courtyard drinking coffee and watching them.

I plunked myself down on a chair. "Enjoying the view, Sir Marcus?"

He glanced over at me before training his gaze back on the ladies. "I am, pretender. You seemed to get off on an interesting foot with Octavia. How is that working out for you?" It seemed Laughlin's best mate didn't like me very much.

"I can assure you, Marc, I am many things, but a pretender isn't one of them. So what's going on? Is there anything I can help with?"

He glared at me and then let out a frustrated sigh. "Look

at her," he indicated Lenore, "she's the most enchanting creature I've ever seen."

It seemed like Cupid's bow was hitting the men hard with the arrival of Suri's tribe. "And there is a problem with this woman of enchantment?" He looked down his nose at me before continuing. "Damn, Laughlin has warned me off. I've got a case of the blue balls I suspect I will have now for several days."

"I'm told she is not what you are usually attracted to, so why this woman? What has she got that is driving you to madness?"

"Her coy smile has driven me over the edge, along with her dimpled cheeks." He scrubbed his face with his hands. "I'm hopelessly in love." His answer surprised me. "I'm told you don't do love, Marcus, and, instead, wine and dine the unsuspecting lasses for a few weeks before you dump them. If you like this woman so much, maybe you could do her a favor and leave her alone? She deserves better, don't you think?"

"Yes, I suppose that is true. You know I had dinner with Suri and Laughlin in Turkey on their first night together. He may not admit it, but he was already smitten with her, and she with him. They just made sense, and even though it was brand new, it seemed like they had always been together. Since then, I have begun to notice how empty my affairs are. The conquests are a game I have thoroughly enjoyed, but I grow tired of the repetitiveness."

It appeared that Marc and I were suffering from the same dilemma. "I understand perfectly, and I have just said to Laughlin that my days of one-night stands with gym girls are over. My thirtieth birthday is next week, and it is time for something more substantial in my life. Someone to enjoy the small things with."

Marcus moved his eyes from Lenore to me. "Funny that we three are the same age. I turn thirty in a few weeks, and I feel the same. I blame Laughlin. After all, if he hadn't found Suri, I would be happily ignorant in my mindless pursuits."

I laughed at that. "Ignorance is bliss."

"And what of you and Octavia? Anything going to happen there?"

"Indeed it will, but for now, I am playing the long game. Octavia knows what type of man I am, and now she needs to come to terms with it. She will come to me. Then she's mine. She just doesn't know it yet."

Chapter 6

Octavia

The drive to the Highlands was annoying, to say the least, and I now understood why Suri had found herself examining her aspects of self. Being sequestered in the studio life, surrounded by people who looked at us as their guru, was a whole lot different than traveling with a bunch of people who didn't know what you were and only a vague sense of who you were. It was humbling, to say the least.

In the front, Laughlin and Suri were in a world of their own, while behind me, Marcus and Lenore were busy casually discussing Scotland and the Highlands. Beside me, Malcolm played on his phone, texting and ignoring me for the most part.

He politely answered questions when asked but didn't activate conversation with me. "You know, you don't have to be petulant, just because I don't want to be your one and only." It was a low blow, but I felt like a boiler that was about to blow.

Malcolm moved his gaze from his phone to me. "I'm sorry, what did you say, Octavia?"

Something inside me snapped, and I had to get out of the vehicle. We were about to pass the dollar cycle trails when I asked for the car to stop.

"Laughlin, please, can you pull over? I need to get out for a moment."

Suri turned around, wearing a look of concern. "O, are you okay?"

I felt tears threatening and knew I needed to get out before making a complete ass of myself. "I'll be fine, just feeling nauseous." I tore out of the SUV and ran for the woods. I ran through the foliage until I was deep enough that no one could see me from the trails if they happened to cycle past.

I dropped down onto a fallen tree limb and let the tears fall. What the hell was wrong with me? I'd been in Scotland only hours, and I was a total mess. I needed to go home. That was the first thought I had. I was safe there, in my cozy studio, tending to my flock. Oh my god, I sounded like a crazy religious leader who'd drunk the Kool-Aid. I cried harder as I realized I wasn't who I thought I was. I heard crunching foliage then, and my head came up from my hands so quickly, my neck snapped.

"What's wrong, lass?"

"Go away, Malcolm."

"No."

"No? Why the hell not? You have been ignoring me since our episode in the bedroom. So continue with that."

"No."

"Seriously?" I said, spinning around to a standing position. "Is that the only word you know? Go away, Malcolm. I won't repeat it."

His eyes glinted with something feral. "For the last time, no, I won't go away. Now tell me what your problem is."

"No! See, I can be as annoying as you. No, no, no," I singsonged as I danced around like the crazy woman I quickly realized I was versus the calm, together yogi I'd been for the last decade.

I was yanked down over Malcolm's knee. "I see you need another lesson in civility. Tsk, tsk, O, you are such a naughty girl."

I was furious at his treatment of me, and yet wasn't it the point of my outburst, to get the great Scotsman's attention? I was incredibly turned on as he yanked my pants down and began delivering hard swats. Acting out as the total brat I was beginning to identify with, I kicked and swore. Then I felt a searing sting across my backside, and I instantly stopped moving as my brain tried to process the sensation. What the? Before I could speak, another horrid sting slashed across my backside. I craned my neck around to see that Malcolm held a thin branch.

"I see I have gained your attention." He brought the tree rod down on my backside with a stinging blow, and I squealed. A dozen later, I was crying for real as I lay draped over his muscular thighs, with all the fight gone.

Malcolm rubbed my ass until I'd calmed down and drew in a few shuddering breaths. He didn't let me up, though, and kept me over his lap as he continued to rub. "Are you ready to have an adult discussion regarding your issue, Octavia?"

"Uh uh," I said, wiping my nose. Malcolm's hand came down hard across the tops of my thighs, and I squealed. "I believe the words you are looking for are, 'yes, sir'."

"Yes, sir," I conceded. Malcolm stood me up and pulled up my pants, then pinned me between his legs. Something about the pose made me feel so vulnerable and gazing almost straight into his eyes because of his seated position, I looked for what I needed, and I saw it there. He was safe. I could drop all my pretenses and share the truth.

Malcolm gazed into my eyes expectantly.

"I will be candid with you. I have been completely unhinged since I met you, and I'm beginning to question everything I knew to be true about myself and what I thought I wanted out of life. I feel lost, and when you ignored me after what we shared, I saw red and was so angry, but that is not me." The understanding in his eyes was almost too much, and I felt the tears pooling again.

"Octavia, I will share a little secret with you that will clear up any confusion." He took my hands in his and kissed each one before riveting his gaze back to mine. "You belong with me. Who you are is a wonderful blend of many magical qualities that I am looking forward to getting to know better. You felt an instant attraction to me when you got off that plane. I saw it in your eyes. Now it is time for you to brave a new version of yourself and realize that I am worth your time, worthy of an investment. Connections like ours are rare and come around, I believe, only once in a life-time. Are you going to pass that up because you're afraid? Because it doesn't fit into the box you have created for yourself?"

He was right, and I was a total idiot. Damn, pheromones had utterly messed with my head.

"You belong to me, my little yogi, for as long as we both decide, understand?"

I nodded my head, feeling like a petulant child. His eyebrows raised with expectation. "Yes, sir." I gave him the proper address he was looking for, and it felt oddly fitting.

"Good girl," he said, drying my cheeks gently. "Let's go, and, Octavia."

"Yes?"

"I warn you now if you are feeling out of sorts and you throw another tantrum today, I will tie you down and whip your ass, got it?" His message was of a severe nature, but his face was smiling. At that moment, the sun found an opening through the tree canopy and shone down on both of us.

I could see the energy in the air, the life force of everything around us, and then when I gazed back at him, I saw Malcolm's was blue with a white ring around it. I knew at that moment that he'd been correct when he'd spoken of our connection. We were meant to be. That thought brought weightlessness to me, and I felt transformed.

Malcolm took my hand and led me back to the vehicle. From the front seat, Suri turned and gazed at me, her unspoken words permeating my consciousness. I smiled in earnest, and she returned it.

"Everything good?" Laughlin, who was not privy to my and Suri's unspoken communiqué, asked.

I gazed at Malcolm and answered, "Everything is perfect."

"Great, then let's get a move on." He pulled back out to the highway, and I spent the rest of the drive holding hands with Malcolm and feeling for the first time in forever, like a woman. Just a woman, and I liked it.

Chapter 7

Laughlin

I checked my phone for a progress report. Adam had sent his jet to New York to pick up two passengers. Dan, his business partner and best friend, and Tsui, whose presence would be my wedding gift to my bride. She had shared how Tsui had born witness to her capture and she would more than likely be dead now if not for him. It seemed fitting that he should witness the next stage in Suri's life and be present at our wedding.

Marcus had been aptly warned about his intentions with Suri's sister, and my brother had proven correct when he said he had everything under control. The woman who had disappeared into the woods was not the same woman who returned. Octavia seemed happy with the outcome of whatever had happened in the woods with Malcolm, the two now cozied up in the middle row of seats.

Suri breathed a sigh of relief, letting go of whatever anxiety she'd been holding since O's arrival at my castle. We pulled onto a non-descript dirt road that sat above the town of Dollar and wound our way up to Castle Gregor.

From the outside, it appeared as a monstrous medieval thing, long deserted. When we pulled up, Adam and Montana were standing on the vast staircase, waiting for us. We piled out of the vehicle, and I heard Octavia say that she couldn't believe how normal they looked. I had to agree with her. Since our return from the Hebrides, I had researched the famous power couple.

I went all the way back to news clippings I'd found of the early band days and even a photo from when Montana was fifteen, exiting a hospital flanked by two men. One was Eddy, and the article said the other was Ace Stanford. Upon further research, I discovered that he was the eldest of the siblings, which explained his eyes. You couldn't make up the crazy story the lovebirds shared. Now that I knew so much more about them, I was looking forward to spending some time in their world.

Unlike Montana and Adam, whose eyes reflected their vast experience with premature age, Ace Stanford's eyes held sorrow. He had been the primary caregiver of his siblings, and I could see his struggles and theirs had profoundly impacted the man. Later that day, I asked Declan about Ace and could tell by his response that he wasn't his favorite person. However, all he said was the man had been given a tough deal.

I was intrigued and wanted to know him better. Suri was introducing Octavia to Adam, and in true Adam style, he peered into eyes like her soul was on display. She must have felt it because she stood still and open to him, not hiding anything. I had to hand it to these yogis. They sure knew how to be in the moment.

We were about to go inside when another car pulled up. Declan jumped out and ran around to the other side, helping a woman out of the vehicle. Skyla was holding onto Declan's hand. He said something, and she blushed prettily. Like Suri, Skyla had darker auburn locks. Unlike Suri, Skyla's locks fell down her back to her ass. She bore herself like Isolde in the tales of Tristan, and something about her seemed very familiar, although I was sure I'd never met the lass. When they spotted us on the stairs, Skyla's eyes sought a friendly face, and when she did, she squealed with excitement, all pretense of ladyship gone from her persona, leaving only an excited long-lost friend. Suri ran down the steps, and the two ladies embraced.

"She is exactly as Suri described her," O said. "They were besties in school. Did you know her, Lenore?" she asked, turning toward Suri's sister.

"No, I really didn't know Mary very well, and certainly none of her friends. She never brought anyone home to meet our parents that I can remember."

Interesting tidbit of information. The ladies walked toward us, with Declan following behind, carrying Skyla's baggage.

When the ladies came back up to the top of the castle steps, Suri made the introductions. Her eyes were shining with sheer happiness and excitement. Then the gaggle of women sped off, with Montana in the lead. I was left with the men, shaking our heads.

"Well, they certainly seem enthusiastic." Adam grinned. "This is nice for Mo. She really likes Suri, and having the ladies here gives her a chance to do women's things."

"That's right, I knew that she grew up without a mother, must have been interesting. I, too, grew up without a mother, mine dying around the same age as Montana's had."

Adam's eyes expanded with interest. "Come, let me show you to your suites, and then we can convene for drinks, lunch, and a tour, sound good?" Then Adam turned to look at

Declan. "Dec, you don't mind bringing in the luggage, do you?"

Declan gave Adam the gimlet-eye, "Aye, fine, but ye better have several drams ready for me when I catch up." Just then, a short woman with a crown of flowing red hair interspersed with gray arrived and looked down the stairs at Declan. "Well, it won't be getting itself moved, will it, son? Hurry up and give your old ma a hug."

Declan rolled his eyes like a kid, eliciting sounds of amusement from those of us still standing on the landing. Adam then headed inside, with the rest of us on his heels. I took one last look at mother and son and then joined the group, leaving them to catch up. The hallways leading off were still in original stone, which made me feel like I'd gone back in time, and to add to that, were two massive tapestries hanging down on either side of the hall. At first, I thought they were left over from the Middle Ages and had miraculously survived. But when I peered up at them closely, I saw that the people portrayed were, in fact, Adam and Montana. I followed the story to the other tapestry and remarked, "This is remarkable work, so old school, yet this is a newly woven tapestry. How on earth did you find someone to make it?"

Adam grinned. "We have a historical textile society in town. Granted, there are only six members, and I hired them to make these two tapestries as an anniversary gift for Montana. They are exquisite, aren't they?"

"Indeed exquisite, miraculous is what I was thinking. This is one of those revitalized businesses you were referring to?"

Adam nodded. "It is, and this castle is an example of ancient knowledge mixed with new technology. Come, Declan is dropping off the luggage, so we can keep going." Adam led us down a hallway that became updated the farther we went. "You see, this castle sits on an old Roman fort, so the fortifications and that of the original castle are far below. We are planning on doing some excavation of the lower levels, as there are several beneath us."

I was shocked. "You're kidding? So, how old is the original structure?"

"Pre-Templars in Scotland, approximately two hundred years prior.

I stopped walking and looked directly into the shorter man's eyes. "You are looking for something?"

Adam smiled. "I am. Declan and Montana came across a secret level when we were secreted here years ago for our protection. My father had gotten a hold of the group who owned the castle at that time, and they put him in touch with Declan's mother. He was living on the back property at that time, in his own place, but Eddy brought him into the fold immediately when introduced to us. Declan's skill set is mad good. Anyway, in the beginning, his job was to be Mo's body-guard. So the two of them spent a lot of time roaming around this castle and found two other levels that no one knew were there. Those levels are not in any set of plans from the past few hundred years. So, either they were kept a secret on purpose, or no one was ever supposed to know those levels were there."

The meaning of his words pierced me like a sword. This could be it. The Templar treasure could be here, hiding just below us. I kept my face blank, covering my excitement. "Do let me know if I can be of assistance. You know that if what you think may be down there is, how this is being handled will be of utmost importance."

Adam glanced back to where Geoff was talking with Sir Henry. "I do, and no one but Declan, Montana, and I know of this."

"Message received," I said, glancing behind me. Reading between the lines, Adam told me he wasn't sure about his father, or maybe he felt his father's intelligence had been hacked. Either way, the less who were privy to the information, the better.

We followed Adam down another hall that led to a row of suites that continued with the repeating theme of old meets new. Adam managed to have the original beds repurposed and had begun a furniture factory specifically for bedrooms in the gothic style. The size of a king-sized bed was double what one would purchase in a store and meant for estate or castle living, not apartments, for apparent reasons.

"Wait until you sleep on them. I'm sure you'll be impressed," Adam said. Our shocked faces must have said it all.

"If the bed is as good as it looks, I will order them for my house. They are remarkable, Adam, your design?"

"Aye, they are, and thank you. We are a word of mouth business because we wouldn't keep up with the demand yet. We still have new graduates training, but it really requires people who have a passion for creating, as these creations are of the non-conveyer belt assembly style."

Malcolm and I stood side-by-side, equally awed by the creative genius giving new life to the impressive antique. "I think just the two of us could keep your company busy for some time," Malcolm added. "I can't wait to lie down on that beauty."

"You mean you can't wait to check out if it makes noise when you rock it," Marcus said, to everyone's laughter.

Malcolm was still mesmerized by the room and, specifically, the bed. "Good question, how solid is it, really? Does it move, squeak?" he asked Adam.

Adam grinned. "You let me know tomorrow." He winked at Malcolm. "Come on, gents, let's go and have that drink."

We followed him along another passage and heard giggling up ahead. We passed what must have been the ballroom, now a sizeable informal family room done up like a coffee lounge, complete with a stage on one end and a vast veranda.

Mrs. C and a few other women I didn't know were in there, along with Montana, Skyla, Lenore, Suri, and O. Ten cackling hens looking at fabrics and flowers and all types of wedding paraphernalia.

"Trust me, brother, you don't want to go in there. I've been here before, and those women will own that room until after the wedding tomorrow," Adam said.

The ladies must have felt our presence because they chose that moment to look up from the extensive fabric choices and give us big smiles.

Two serving women pushed us out of the way as they brought in trays of foods for the women. "That's our cue. Looks like our lunch is waiting for us," Adam said, leading us to the dining room off the kitchen.

I poked my head in the kitchen as we passed. "You haven't updated it. Is that a future project?"

Adam laughed, "Only if Mrs. C allows it. She says this is her room and to leave it as it is. As she has taken such good care of this place and my family, what Mrs. C wants, Mrs. C gets."

I thought of Annie. Even as my father's lover, I didn't remember a time when he'd given her any considerations. I was his son and spent much time alone, with zero regard to my wishes and thought that Annie must have gone mad from my father's ignorance of her needs. "You're a good man, Adam Northrop."

"So I'm told, seems to be my cross to bear. Right this way."

An odd thing to say but, Adam Northrop was no ordinary man. Even I, with my great capacity for control and investigation, couldn't have taken on the Stanford family, most significantly, not Montana.

We took our seats, pairing off naturally in conversation. Declan had arrived and was speaking with my brother about his gyms. Geoff and Henry seemed to be old friends despite only meeting two days ago. Marcus was gazing off into space, looking like he had something on his mind.

"Have you heard when Tsui and your brother-in-law will arrive?"

"I have, tomorrow around lunch, but as you requested, Tsui's presence remains a surprise until the wedding. I thought to have a separate meal from the ladies, who will undoubtedly be busy in wedding mode anyway. And a surprise guest, Ace, Mo's eldest brother. I know you wanted to meet him, so I invited him to join us."

I would get to meet the eldest Stanford, and for some reason, that excited me. I felt somehow that he was the key, but I hadn't yet deciphered as to what.

Chapter 8

Malcolm

A dam and my brother had been talking in hushed tones for quite some time. I wondered what they were up to, but more than that, I tried to imagine what my sweet O was doing. After lunch, I ducked out of the rest of the castle tour and made my way back to the giant commons room where the ladies had been earlier.

The room was empty except for two seamstresses and Suri. I licked my lips in anticipation of hunting down Octavia. Going by instinct, I made my way back down the hallway of suites Adam had toured us by a few hours before. They had numbers listed on the doors, and I made my way to lucky number 8. I had no idea if it was hers, but I would soon find out.

I stood at the door, listening for a moment, and then silently turned the knob and cracked open the door. I was right. This was O's room, in which she was presently engaged in doing yoga, no doubt stiff after the long plane ride and then the car ride and, of course, not to mention the two spankings she'd already received from me.

She was almost naked, doing yoga in her boy shorts and tank top. The room was vast, as they all were, and she had plenty of room to work out in front of the massive windows where the curtains were thrown wide open. O's view was of endless rolling hills, which were beautiful but not nearly as eye-catching as her toned body.

I found myself mesmerized by her fluid motions. My brother was right; yoga was a discipline that looked easy, like dancing, but I knew the movements she was doing took great skill, especially to perform as well as she was.

My cock grew painfully stiff in my pants as I watched her bend forward and step back into some inverted V pose that had her ass high in the sky. When her panties slid up, little pink lines, the remnants of her recent birching in the forest, were evident.

Unintentionally, I growled, alerting my perfect yogi to my presence. Still in that deep V pose, she gazed through her legs at me.

"Don't you dare move," I said, entering her room and locking the door behind me.

I walked behind her and undid my trousers, then plunged into her warmth. We both moaned with the intensity of our flesh connecting so profoundly. I got a firm grip on her hips, alleviating the weight from her arms, and took her hard and fast. This was not to be a long, drawn-out lovemaking session. This was pure fucking, out of a desperate need to feel each other.

Together, we moved closer to the edge and flung ourselves off at the same time, our mutual orgasms gripping us in waves of pleasure. O's spasming walls milked the most prolonged release I ever remembered having. Once our bodies stopped trembling, I scooped her into my arms and deposited her on the mammoth-sized bed.

"I'm told these beds don't make a sound. If proven accurate, I'm buying one."

O gazed up into my eyes. "Really, I can't wait for you to recover so we can test out the theory."

I grinned at her and pulled her in tighter in our frontal spoon position. "How are you enjoying castle life?"

"Honestly, this entire trip has been surreal. Yet so real that I feel like my life until I arrived in Scotland was a dream or haze. It's weird, but I'm beginning to understand what Suri said when I arrived this morning."

"Oh, and what was that?"

"She thought she was truly living, alive in every sense of the word, before she met Laughlin. After spending a few hours with him and in his world, she quickly realized that she had only ever devoted herself to the petals of awakening, not to the root that created the flower in the first place. Laughlin, apparently, brings out the best of both her natures."

"I see, and you understand that better now than when you arrived. Why?"

A gentle blush moved across her cheeks. "Because, silly, of what you said to me in the woods. Everything you said was right, and I realized that I've lived in a box of my own creation. Under the pretense of that being what I wanted, and in truth, yoga is what I needed. But also because I couldn't see anything else for me. I'm almost thirty-two years old, Malcolm, and I have never had a great love or lover. I devoted myself to education and then a corporate job in Australia. Yoga took me over about a decade ago, and I have been in the chrysalis ever since. I feel like I have finally emerged from the cocoon and am seeing the real world for the first time."

She nestled into my chest like she belonged there, and it felt so right. With her, it was hard to imagine a life that didn't have O in it. Yet up until a few hours ago, that was precisely what I'd been living.

"I feel the same way. In fact, my life, until a few months ago, was a lie, and in the past forty-eight hours has taken an entirely new development. Seeing my brother with Suri, I was reminded how empty my life has been. I am turning thirty next week, and like you, O, have never had a great anything, lover or partner. Suri is so different than any woman I'd ever met, and I was envious of my brother for finding a woman who didn't seem to suffer from things that gym women tend to suffer from. Then, voila, you came along, a white rose, so many petals for me to expose, and so much depth for me to lose myself in. You indeed are perfect, Octavia."

She giggled. "Hardly. I have realized, like my bestie, that I am more of a brat than I realized."

I squeezed her ass hard, eliciting a yelp from her perfect mouth. "Aye, ye are a brat, and that is also perfect. Because I love spanking the brattiness out of you." I turned her around and pressed my hard cock against her little tight backside bud. "Feel that, O, that is what happens to me when I picture you over my lap."

She nestled back against my cock, and then drawing one knee up to her ear, she reached back and grabbed it, moving my hardened length to her weeping channel.

"Feel that, Malcolm, that is what happens to me when I think of you spanking my naughty backside."

I groaned as I thrust into her, this time keeping my strokes torturously slow. I used one hand to hold her hip, and the other alternated between her pert breasts and rose pink nipples.

She moaned in my mouth as I tweaked her nipples, and a gush covered my cock. She was already responding to me with such passion. It was like her body was made for pleasure and mine for delivering it. When I felt her next wave approaching,

I slapped her mons. O squealed with shock in my mouth and was ready for the next one as she released her essence and didn't stop. I kept tapping her clit, and she came undone with every single one. When I'd wrung multiple orgasms out of her body, I increased the speed of my pumps, holding her tight and finally letting go, filling her with my seed and thankful the woman was on birth control as she'd told me earlier, because I was sure if she hadn't been, this session would have had her with child.

I rolled onto my side, taking her with me. "I've never been to Australia. What's it like?"

"Well, it's beautiful. I grew up in a small town toward the northern end. The country is very rugged when you're not in the cities and larger towns. Did you know your country used to send prisoners there a few hundred years ago? It is a perfect prison island. However, in the larger cities, it's just like anywhere else. I worked in tech in both Sydney and Brisbane after graduation. Sydney reminds me of Vancouver, where our hosts are from. Have you been?"

I shook my head. "I have been all over Europe, but I have not been to Canada or Australia."

"You'd love Vancouver. It gets almost as much rain as Scotland." She laughed. "Montana was telling us that her brother still lives in the house they grew up in, and when her parents bought it, the west end of Vancouver, where she is from, was teaming with Europeans."

That was interesting. I really didn't know anything about our hosts other than she was a singer and he was an artist. Almost as if O had read my mind, she said, "Have you noticed the art in this castle? I'll bet it's worth a fortune."

"Do you like art, Octavia?"

"Yes, I do, and it is on my to-do list to get to Ash Lane in Glasgow. I hear there is a fine gallery, and the neighborhood boasts many local artists."

"I own a small gym on that street. It's not traditional, like my others, and set up for calisthenics. You're right about there being many artists in the neighborhood, and they like to stay in shape, but they don't like a lot of equipment. Are you familiar with calisthenics?"

"Vaguely, they use bars and their own body weight for the workout, which is very similar to yoga. The big difference is yoga has choreography, with a purpose, a set of motions that all have a point, either in holding or transitioning. I think that's why I like it so much. There is a continuity that is missing for me in traditional workouts. Even your calisthenics is missing the flow from one thing to the next. I believe you guys do counts or timing for each pose and then move on to the next. So what happens between the poses?"

"I'm not sure what you mean by between the poses."

"Okay, watch." Octavia sprang out of bed and to the floor. I rolled up onto my elbow so I could watch what she was doing. She was completely naked by now, and I was more excited by that than whatever she was about to do until she started moving.

"Okay, so here is the plank pose. I will hold it for thirty seconds. Now watch. I'm going into down dog and walking back, so my weight is only on my feet. From there, I will widen my legs and fold up into a squat and do eight. Then I will walk back out into down dog and do pike push-ups. I'm going to walk back and repeat the squats, then I'm going to walk out and do plank push-ups."

I watched as she transitioned from one to the other without ever moving from her spot. I felt my eyes widen as I saw the possibilities unfold before my eyes. When she was done, she was sweating, and it had only been ten minutes, but it had been a full-on ten minutes without stopping, to move to a new spot or think her next exercise. Her body just flowed from one to the other.

"Can you teach me?" I jumped up, and she coached me through the routine. I was tight and found the transitions challenging to perform. That was the point. That transition was part of the practice, not something one stopped to do. When I was done, I sat on the floor, breathing hard, like I'd just done a full-on workout.

"O, that was brilliant. I learned something today. Maybe you could do what you just did for my chain and teach yoga calisthenics so I could offer it at my studios? But with clothes on, of course."

"Yes, but after my European tour. I want a break from business and from teaching. I need to spread my wings."

"Oh? How about spreading your legs and flying free instead?" I yanked her legs apart and dove between them, greedily sucking on her. Her taste was a blend of me, salt, sweat, and essence, which reminded me of sweet nectar. Not until I brought her to the cusp and over the edge several times, did I help her rise up from the floor.

I checked my phone. Two hours had passed, and I was now in desperate need of a shower. I wondered where my room was and if I could sneak out of O's and into mine without being seen.

"O, you don't happen to know my room number, do you?"

She grinned. "You're in it, handsome. I passed Declan when he brought up the luggage and told him to put yours here with mine. I hope you don't mind?"

"Mind? You just saved me from having to tiptoe naked down the hall. Thank you, lass. Come on, let's go shower. I want to wash that gorgeous body of yours."

"I'll take you up on that. It's been a while since I've been washed."

I felt a growl in my throat rise, unbidden. My alpha male was having issues with the knowledge that anyone had washed my woman. I gripped O's hair in my fist, keeping her from moving. "Who?"

As she was facing me, I could watch her expressions. She wasn't intimidated in the least, but she was very turned on. "I'm sorry, who, what?"

I gripped her hair tighter and watched as she winced and then her pupils dilated. "You know what I'm asking you, little yoga brat, now answer the question."

She grinned. "My first fuck if you must know. But it wasn't romantic. It was because I was paranoid and thought my parents would know, so we showered at his place, and I went home."

I released her hair. "And that's the only time?"

"It is. You're not jealous of my past, are you?"

"No, O, I'm not jealous, just want a list of all the ways I need to mark my territory until all of your memories of sex are replaced with new ones with me."

"Well then," she husked, "we'd better get started."

By the time I was done marking my territory, we were starving and surprised when we heard a knock on our door announcing dinner in half an hour.

"Malcolm, what do I wear? I haven't dined in a castle before. Is there a dress code?"

For some reason, the question made me think of Suri and my brother. I'll bet he guided her a lot with her outfit choices. "May I see the selection and choose something for you?"

For the first time since the car, Octavia wore a look of uncertainty. "Uh, you can, but, well, I am a minimalist and don't have a lot to choose from. Don't laugh, but I fit almost my entire wardrobe in that backpack when I packed for this trip."

I liked the minimalist aspect of her personality. I wouldn't have to worry when buying her gifts that she may already have what I selected, or something similar. I went through her meager wardrobe and was happy to see that the fabrics she chose to wear were super soft and would form to her perfectly sculpted body.

I found a light pink bodysuit that looked like a bra on top but had a piece of material that ran from the center down, into pants, so the sides of her waist were visible but not her tummy. The legs were wide and flowing and appearing like a skirt. I handed her the jumper and a thong, but no underwear. A bra wouldn't work with the jumper, but as it offered its own support, she wouldn't need one.

Then I found her one pair of dressy shoes that offered an open toe and a two-inch heel and handed those to her, along with a scarf for her shoulders. Then I went looking through her jewelry options and found one of those beaded things that Suri always wore, and it was in moonstone. I grabbed the strand of beads and handed it to her.

When she was done, I changed out the scarf for a bolero shoulder jacket that matched her shoes. She put on the mala beads, which I learned was the name, around her neck, but I asked her to wind them around her wrist instead, and it completed the look. She gazed in the mirror at the finished product and liked what she saw. "Remind me to get you to dress me whenever we go out. You really have an eye for fashion."

"No, not fashion, bodies, and I could see this on your body. Besides, I have something to match." I drew out of the closet my tan slacks and pearl pink dress shirt and rolled up the sleeves. Instead of the jacket, I placed a cable knit across my shoulders and matching shoes. O and I stood staring at ourselves in the mirror.

"We look perfect," she uttered quietly, "like a couple."

"Like it was meant to be?" I found her eyes in the mirror's reflection.

"Yes, just like that, but it seems so unreal. Malcolm, is this real?"

"As real as us standing here, O. My brother told me that on his first night with Suri, they went to dinner with Marcus and his date at that time. Marcus told me that they were already a couple, they just didn't know it yet. Fate, O, brought them together, just like it has for us. Don't question it; just enjoy it."

She smiled in the mirror. "Okay, I can do that. One day at a time, right?"

"Exactly. Do what all you yogis boast about, stay present. Anxiousness comes with expectation, does it not?"

Her eyes rounded, and she nodded her head. Then she turned to me and gazed into my eyes directly. O seemed small and vulnerable at that moment. "Malcolm, I need you to grant me a favor, please."

"Of course, name it."

"Please, whatever happens, if we end up together or not, just please don't hurt me. I'm falling so hard, and I'm afraid."

I pulled her in tight and kissed her deeply. "I promise you, O, that if we part, it will be because you choose it, not because of something I've done."

She smiled, and when she did, her light parted the darkness that had momentarily taken over. As we walked to dinner, I prayed that I could keep my promise.

Chapter 9

Suri

I didn't know why I was so nervous. But my heart was racing so fast that even meditative breathing wasn't helping me. It was four hours until the wedding, and the panic had set in. I needed to go swimming, and Montana said they had a pool.

Throwing on a bathing suit and one of Laughlin's long shirts, I went in search of the pool. I didn't want to ask anyone, as I didn't want anyone to see me. I was waging a battle that I was sure anyone would know if I stopped to ask for directions. I was approaching another hallway when I saw Adam step out of his office.

He gave me that soul-searching look, and that was all it took. I fell apart. "Suri, is there something I can do for you?"

"I... was looking for the pool," I garbled through my tears. "Can you direct me? Please, I need some—"

"Freedom?" Adam said gently. All I could do was nod my head. "Then you need more than the pool, lass, come with me." Adam led me down a flight of stone stairs and out a door somewhere behind the castle.

We walked through a field, toward a forested area. We didn't speak, and I was happy to let him lead and follow quietly behind. When we stepped through the glen, we were in a magical place. It was a lagoon, sparkling in the sunshine, the water looking like a treasure.

"This is incredible."

"It is. Montana and I and her twin Alex came here when we needed some healing, and this was where we found it."

I took off my shirt and waded in. The water was warm, which was surprising. I turned a quizzical look on Adam, who said it was a hydrothermal spring.

"Adam, are you coming in?"

"No, but I will be here to make sure you are safe and walk you back to the castle."

I felt a sense of profound relief at his words. Adam remaining with me, would allow me to completely relax and not worry about someone spying on me, or worse. Closing my eyes allowed me to feel my tensions melt away, replaced with soothing warmth. I could feel the earth beneath my feet. It spoke to me of its ancientness and fed me energy. I felt and saw it as it rose around me.

I began to hum the Soham mantra, and then my voice joined in as the words poured forth from me. I didn't feel shy around Adam. He was like a part of the journey, a part of the energy in this place. I dove to the lagoon's bottom and held myself on the bottom as long as I could. And although I was sure only seconds had passed, it felt like long minutes as I became the lotus flower, sinking my roots deep in the darkness below.

I felt my divinity, my connection to the universe, to God, to nature, to all things energy. And when I came back up and passed through the surface of the water, I felt different. Gone was all the anxiousness of earlier, the hesitations that humans, in general, experience. I pulled myself up onto a rock in the sunshine beside Adam.

He smiled in a knowing way that told me he completely understood what I had just gone through. We sat in silence for minutes. How many, I couldn't say.

"Adam, Montana told me that you have been doing yoga since you were a teenager. May I ask what the draw for you at that time was?"

He smiled at me, and I was hit again with his unique, special force. Adam was a mystery, with a gentle soul. "I feel like you are a kindred spirit, a person who is deeply connected to what life is truly about."

"High praise indeed. But I will tell you, my motivation for yoga when I began was to let go of my sexual frustrations. You see, I knew of Montana since she was thirteen, when I met her brother Dan. I watched her from afar, her mistakes, her injuries, her incredible spirit. She moved me. But she was too young for me to approach. When she was fifteen, I followed her one night to the movies. She was there alone, and from plying Dan with questions, I knew that late-night films down on the notorious Granville Street were forbidden to her. But Montana always did what she wanted."

I laughed, imagining the same woman as a girl getting into constant trouble. "I guess she was a handful, so you made sure she got home safely?"

He nodded, a shadow passing over his face. "Ace and Dan have arrived, so you will get to meet her older brothers. It's an interesting dynamic. I was on my way to greet them when you came down the hall."

"Oh, I'm sorry, but I'm not. This is exactly what I needed."

"Aye, it was, but in answer to your original question, watching that little minx, had me turned on all the time. Add in that she is my muse and I spent long hours drawing and painting her, with a constant hard-on. I needed some peace, some Zen."

I laughed so hard at his earnestness, and he joined me. "Thank you, Adam, for bringing me here and sharing with me. I truly appreciate it." He nodded his head like karma acts were a constant in his life, and scrutinizing him, I realized they probably were. I wished he and Tsui could meet. I imagined that they would get on superbly.

"Adam, I know you are taking photos of the wedding for us, and I am so grateful. But I was wondering, when you have time, one day, if I may commission you to do a painting from today?"

Adam rose and held out his hand to help me up. When I took it, I felt a spark of energy, like Adam had living, thriving energy pulsating through his veins. "Done, and don't worry about commissioning me. It will be a gift."

"No, I couldn't possibly. You have given so much already. I mean, this place, it is magical, and I am so honored that you shared it with me."

"You gave me something just as magical when you healed my wife. Montana seems like a new woman. Her injury was so long ago. In fact, the stab wound was before we were dating. But it was a catalyst for us to move to the next stage. My father paid for her hospital bill and her subsequent months of therapy. Anyway, I forgot what she was like before the stab wound, and I noticed the shift in her after your work. It's like she is lighter, or some invisible shackles have been lifted. She said she has never felt better, and for that reason alone, I would paint you a hundred portraits."

I was embarrassed by his praise. Sophie and Montana were the only two people I had done reiki on since I left New York. Well, except the assassin on the beach in Greece. Needless to say, I hadn't had much practice.

Adam broke my thoughts, "Are you ready to go back?"

"I am, thank you." The two of us walked back to the castle in companionable silence, and when we were back at the hallway that went to our suites, Adam wished me luck and disappeared around a corner. I entered our room and sank into the divan, still musing over my time in the lagoon, when I heard a knock on my door.

"Come in."

Montana poked her head in. "Is it safe to enter?"

I laughed at her expression. "If you're wondering if Laughlin is wandering around naked, then, yes, it's safe."

"Good," she said, opening the door fully and coming inside. "I ran into Adam as I was escaping my brothers. He said he took you to the lagoon. What did you think?"

"Escaping?"

"You first, Suri."

"Magical, and perfect, just what I needed. Now your turn."

"Ugh," she said, slamming into the back of the chaise she now sat on with me. "I love them dearly, but they drive me crazy. 'Montana, you're too skinny.' 'Montana, what have you been up to?' 'Montana, you know you need to stay hydrated; drink some water.'" I laughed at her impersonation of the men I hadn't met yet.

"Adam said you shared an interesting dynamic with your older brothers, but not your twin?"

"No, Alex and I are different. He can see inside my head, so he knows what I'm all about. Those guys can't see inside my head, so they judge me by my actions, or lack of."

"What do you mean by seeing inside your head? You mean because you are twins, he knows you better?"

"No. I mean, literally, Alex can enter my brain. I can send him signals, but rarely have I been able to do the same to him. Mind you, I have also learned how to block him out. He hates that." She laughed mirthlessly. Changing the subject abruptly, she said, "I heard you want me to sing as you walk down the aisle?"

I blushed furiously. "Well, I would love it, but I didn't ask because you are already doing so much."

She waved her hand in the air as she uttered, "Tsk, it's nothing. Now, do you have a song in mind, or would you like me to pick one?"

It was my turn to slam my head back into the divan. "Honestly, all I really want is natural and organic everything. I want you to pick, and I want you to pick what feels right to you. This wedding is just a formality for Laughlin and me. But being here, celebrating with only a few close friends, is exactly what I wanted."

"I understand. When Adam and I decided to get married here in Scotland, my brothers were motivated and asked if I minded sharing the limelight with them. Which, of course, I didn't, so we all got married at the same ceremony in our chapel. There were more brides and grooms than guests."

"Oh my god, seriously; that's different."

"It is, with no one to babysit on our anniversaries, we didn't think that one through, though. Now, we have two hours until showtime. Mrs. C and Colleen will be here shortly with refreshments. I can't have you fainting. They will help you dress, so you need to shower now, and I need to go check on a few things. I'll be back, and then we will make our way to the chapel."

I stood up on shaking legs. This was it, the final count-down. Montana and I hugged, and then she left. I took a nice hydrotherapy shower that woke me up from my lagoon stupor. I threw on a robe just in time as Mrs. C and Colleen came in carrying an assortment of items, with Octavia on their heels.

"Well, halo, lassie, are ye ready for yer final fitting?" I couldn't help but like Declan's mother. She was the epitome of what every person wanted in a mother.

"Yes, and thank you again for all your help."

She waved her hand and tsked exactly like Montana, and now I knew where she had gotten it. "First, you need a snack, lass, something to fortify you, aye?" She poured a strong cup of tea and handed it to me. I took a sip and hummed in appreciation. Next, she gave me a cookie that tasted a lot like a protein bar. "Aye, she answered to my query, "it is something that Daniel told me about. Apparently, he lived on protein bars in Canada while he was in school."

I smiled and stored that tidbit of information for when I was to meet the older Stanford men.

"Now, lass, go and brush your teeth. You don't want to be doing that after the lipstick, aye?"

I followed Mrs. C's orders without argument, and after the final fitting, they removed the dress and sat me in a chair centered in a pool of light pouring in through the vast picture windows. "We'll be back shortly to help you into your gown. Ms. Octavia said she will do your make-up and hair first."

On that note, the other two women left, and the room stilled as if a hush descended after they were gone.

"Are you ready, Suri?"

I took O's hands. "I am. We haven't had much time to talk, but tell me, how is it going with Malcolm?"

O brought over the stacks of make-up and brushes and began on my face, wearing a small wistful smile all the while. "It is perfect, Suri. I totally get what you meant by you weren't what you thought you were. I've been having one epiphany after the other about myself since I got off the plane yesterday morning. I can't believe what my life has been in twenty-four hours."

I chuckled. "I know the feeling. Running for my life into the arms of Laughlin was like a dream. Well, literally, as I told you, I'd seen him in my dream before I left New York. I'm glad for you that you have found an equal."

O's brow furrowed slightly. "We're not equals, not yet at any rate. That wily Scotsman is always one step ahead of me. Stop laughing, or you'll screw up the mascara!"

"I can't help it. I have never known anyone to be one step ahead of you, Octavia."

"Yeah, well, I found that *someone*, but it works for me, to my surprise. I like the not knowing. I like it a lot. The instability of surprise brings with it a freshness that I was desperately craving but didn't know. I've been hiding for ten years, and I didn't know that, either. Imagine if your yoga journey had been ten years instead of one."

"I think I would be struggling way more than you are, my friend."

O laughed at my response. "You think? I don't. You seem to embrace your life so vibrantly, Suri. I have never seen you this alive, not even after that transformation class on Bhastrika."

"Mmm, that was the best master class ever, seeing Sri Babba and knowing he had arrived to lead me into the deeper realms. But you're right. My meeting Laughlin and having what we have is incomparable."

O stopped painting my face and looked at me in the mirror. "Can I ask you something personal?"

"Of course, you know you can ask me anything."

"Laughlin is very dominant."

"Is that a question or a statement?"

"I'm not finished, smarty pants. I mean, Laughlin being dominant, is it more than in the sack?"

"He has been overly dominant since we met because of the circumstances of how that happened. The mystery is still afoot, and there are still two large missing pieces of information. I think when that is solved and the players found, he will be less so. However, I fell in love with him just as he is. If it doesn't change, that's okay. I do get to play some wonderful bratty games."

I wondered if our peals of laughter could be heard out in the hall. When we calmed down, I asked about Malcolm.

"He likes to be in control, but he is far from a control freak. He needs to lead, direct, and maybe he would be dominant if my life were in danger or someone close to him."

"Yeah, well, you haven't met his mother. After you do, your life may be endangered. I'm telling you, that woman is deranged and is very possessive of Malcolm. Her hate for Laughlin is palpable, even though he is innocent of what happened with Annie, Malcolm's mother."

"Hmm, I will have to ask more about that later. I'm intrigued and wondering how this situation you have alluded to will play out when all is said and done."

"If things get said and done, I pray this Templar mystery and our connection to it gets worked out."

"Me too. Now, about Malcolm... he has impeccable taste. He is smart, educated, and successful. But most importantly, he sees me."

I rolled my eyes at her ignorance, the rose-colored glasses mode she was in. I knew Malcolm. He was way more dominant than she was giving him credit for. "Yes, these Campbell men tend to see their women, don't they?"

O nodded. "So your sister, Lenore, she seems like she has been very sheltered."

"I suppose we were definitely raised a certain way, and both of us did what was expected. I think Lenore is still doing our parents' bidding."

"And Marcus?"

"Oh my god, can you imagine? If she fell for him and he dumped her, which he would, I would never hear the end of it."

"You don't think he can change? He seems pretty smitten with her."

"Yeah, probably because he hasn't had her yet. It's been three days, and Marcus usually has his conquests well under his spell in the first hour he meets them. Enough about them, have you met Montana's brothers? I heard they arrived while I was swimming."

O nodded. "I did, and the middle one, Dan? He is gorgeous, reminds me of Montana's husband. The older one, is… I don't know, repressed? Dark? He's gotta be close to forty but looking into his eyes… he reminds me of a soldier after the war, those young men with haunted looks."

I was intrigued. From a healer's perspective, I wondered if Ace Stanford was someone I could help. I was lost in my thoughts on Montana and her clan of brothers when O said, "Earth to Suri, we are done."

I refocused my eyes and took a look at myself. Octavia had done an outstanding job. My eyes really caught in the light and looked emerald-green instead of their usual mossy color. "Wow, thank you." I stood and stretched when there was a knock on the door.

Mrs. C was back. "Now, lass, we have just enough time to get you in that dress and over to the chapel."

"Mrs. C, is everything ready? Have you seen the chapel?"

"Aye, lass, all is ready and looks almost as beautiful as you." She clucked her tongue. "Montana decided it was best to stay where she was to prepare, so it's just us three, aye."

When I was ready, we three ladies made our way to the chapel. I stood inside the entrance behind the wall and listened to the voices. I was so nervous, and I hoped Laughlin loved the dress. I went for the mermaid dress in plaid. It was daring, but I wanted to wear Laughlin's colors, and I knew the style would show off my hourglass figure splendidly.

The box music that had been playing stopped, a guitar

started, and then Montana's melodic, haunting voice rang out. Octavia made her way around the wall and began her elegant walk to the front of the chapel. I swallowed the lump in my throat and followed her. When I came around the corner, the first thing I saw was all of the flowers.

The fragrance hit me, and I literally stopped in my tracks to take a deep breath, to the chuckles of everyone in the room. With a grin on my face, I continued down the walk until I stood beside Laughlin. He was in full Highland regalia and looked delicious. My senses were aware that Adam was taking photos, Montana was singing, and there were guests in the room, friends old and new.

But all that paled in comparison to the lord I was about to marry. I glanced to my left at Octavia, who smiled encouragingly. My eyes traveled past Laughlin to his brother Malcolm, whose gaze was set firmly on my best friend. In that moment, the energy in the room shifted and I knew there would be another wedding, and soon.

The preacher took us through the steps, and then it was time for our vows. Mine was almost word for word what I'd said to Octavia yesterday morning.

Then it was Laughlin's turn. "Suri, as you know, I am a man who has spent most of his life alone, always in training for a greater purpose than my own desire or comfort. I closed the door to finding a mate, a match. I never thought such a thing was possible. But when you ran into me, lass, I was hit with a miracle, a blessing that I will never take for granted. I love you, and I'm still learning all the ways a man can love a woman. I respect your person, as you are the most remarkable human being I have ever met. I trust you with my heart, my home, and myself. You feed my soul and love the dominant man I am. I will spend the rest of my life showing you that by picking me, you made the right choice."

It was a lot for someone like Laughlin to say out loud or

share among friends, as he was such a private person. I was moved by his willingness to share his heart in front of others. When we slid the rings on each other's fingers, I felt the seal, the bond of matrimony, wrap its way around my finger and my heart.

We turned to the cheers of those who had been silent behind us, and it was then I noticed a surprise guest, Tsui Tran. When our eyes connected, a big smile lit my face. My second bestie had made it. I turned to Laughlin, "Oh, thank you, Loc, this means so much."

He smiled indulgently at me. "Well, I couldn't let the one person responsible for your rescue not be here for you, lass. But you could have told me."

"Told you what?"

"Well, that he's a very handsome man for one, but that he is a Templar."

The shock must have been evident, "Not now, lass, close those beautiful lips, let go, and greet everyone by the way. I'll do my best not to tear that dress off you later. My cock has been straining under my kilt to plunder you, damn woman. You look perfect in my plaid colors."

I giggled. "I know what you mean. I feel the same way about you in that get-up. You have to promise to wear it on every anniversary. I want to be taken by my Highland lord."

His eyes darkened dangerously. "I think I can accommodate that."

As we walked down the aisle toward the light of the entrance, every person I knew and cared about was here with me, and my heart was brimming with love. I hugged everyone, including Montana's two brothers, whom I hadn't met yet. When I hugged Ace, I searched and found remorse, and when I pulled back, he gazed at me with a look that said he knew I'd just done something. However, now was not the time, as

Laughlin was impatient to get the pictures done and then move back into the castle for dinner.

"Tsui." I ran into his embrace outside the chapel. "I can't believe you're here. How did you manage it?"

"Suri, beautiful soul, how are you? I didn't manage it, your friend Adam did, and I flew over here with his brothers-in-law."

"Oh?" I pulled Tsui off to the side. "Weird energy, don't you think?" Tsui knew who I was talking about. "Yes, he is carrying a heavy burden."

"I think we could help him."

"Well, we could, if that is what he wants."

"Right." I took a deep breath. "I'm so glad you're here, Tsui. You have met everyone?"

"I have."

"And? Come on, what do you think of Laughlin?"

Tsui's face remained the same, but his energy shifted. "I think many things, something specific you are looking for, moon goddess?"

I wanted to sigh in exasperation, but the coy look he was giving me made me laugh.

Then arms were wrapping around me from behind. "There you are, beauty."

Tsui reached out his hand and shook Laughlin's. "Congratulations, Mr. Campbell."

"Thank you, Tsui, or do you still go by your Templar name, Lord Rothley?"

Tsui regarded Laughlin, his face not changing in the slightest with the accusation. "I left my titles and connections behind, Lord Roswell, when I went to the Tibetan monastery. I am as you see, and nothing more."

"Are you? Then you have nothing to do with the Sinclairs or Suri's trip to Turkey." Silence permeated our space and the intensity, blocking out the sounds from those around us.

"If you are asking me if I knew of Mary's identity when she came to New York, the answer is yes. If you're asking me if I kept a watch on her because I had insider information about what was going on with her husband, father-in-law, and the company, then the answer is yes. Beyond that, I know nothing."

I was in shock. All this time, Tsui had been a Templar. He knew of my ex-husband, his father, and my father. How was it possible that Tsui had become one of my best friends and I hadn't learned this rather important fact about him?

"Lord Rothley? So you are Scottish too?"

"English, but I do have roots in Scotland."

"Uh, if you'll excuse me, I think I need to get a drink." I left the two men facing off. This couldn't be happening. Why was nothing as it seemed in my life? I wondered about my sister. Was she really here for my wedding, or was she a spy sent to be an informant? I gazed around me as I followed the group to the castle, wondering if, like everything else in my life, Laughlin and I were a lie.

Chapter 10

Laughlin

"What the hell is going on?" Geoff, Sir Henry, and Malcolm came upon Tsui and me.

"Ask him," I said, pointing accusingly at Tsui, aka Lord Rothley.

Tsui released his eye contact with me and took a step back. "It seems Lord Roswell has an issue with my old identity, and I think it's time for me to leave, as this blessed event is about the union of two people, and one of them is very upset and alone right now."

"He's right, Laughlin, Montana and O are with your bride, trying to cheer her up on her wedding day. Whatever this is, it can't be any worse than what I did, so let it rest, and we will figure it out later," Malcolm said.

My brother was right. I was charging like a headstrong bull, which was very unlike me. "You are correct. My apologies, Tsui. I don't know what came over me. Shall we go inside for the festivities? I need to find Suri and apologize."

Tsui uttered, "Of course."

Geoff, Sir Henry, and Tsui walked ahead of Malcolm and me to the castle, giving me time to take some deep breaths.

"What is going on?"

"That man isn't Tsui Tran."

Malcolm dared to laugh. "I assumed, brother. After all, he is very English, isn't he?"

I rolled my eyes. "Yes, he is quite white, as you say, but that's not what I mean. What I mean is he is a Templar and a Rothley. And the last I heard, Rothley's heir disappeared, yet here he is at my wedding and best friends with my wife. Do you see my issue?"

"Not entirely. Is this Lord Rothley a bad person? Has he been connected with the powers who are causing issues for the Templars?"

"Well, no."

"Then the only problem here is you being jealous of that gorgeous blond surfer-looking yogi who happens to care about Suri. Best get over that, brother. I'm beginning to realize that these yogis have their own philosophy and care deeply for each other."

Damn Malcolm for being the wise one, even if he was older by a few months. I felt my experience and education should have given me superior intuition, but he was right, and I was wrong in this case. And then I remembered why I never had relationships. They dull your senses. Was this the beginning of me losing my edge? Not wishing for another lecture from my slightly older brother, I kept my thoughts to myself.

I painted a smile on my face and went in search of Suri when we reached the castle. I found her drinking and laughing with the women. She had been crying, I could tell, and she was hurting and covering it up. I could tell that too. I was such an asshole. How could I be so mean? I decided the best way to make up for what I'd done, was to apologize to Tsui in front of Suri and then beg for her forgiveness.

"Tsui, please, I need to fix this with Suri. Will you come with me so I can formally apologize to you both? I really don't know what came over me, and I'm a little out of my element at the moment."

"Of course, I will, Laughlin, and I'm not offended in the least. You felt the need to protect her. That is your love and your alpha archetype telling you to protect your home and family. You are a wolf, and Suri is now your mate. You would do anything for her, even humble yourself to make things right with her."

I stopped walking and looked at the yogi with new eyes of appreciation. "You are correct. Thank you for putting it so plainly. I was beginning to wonder other things."

"Like if you're good enough for her? If being in a relationship was a mistake, if you're losing your edge?"

I was shocked at his words. "How the hell did you know that?"

"Laughlin, do you find it impossible to lie to Suri? She can see you clearly, no matter what? That is a learned thing from working with me. She can see who you are, and she loves the man you are. That is more than most people can say. Very few of us experience love for what it is and even less, see our mate's true self. You are a lucky man in that you have both with her. She is lucky because you see her in all her glory, her petals, and her root. That's what her marriage vows were about. They were brilliant, don't you think? She said you brought her pieces together and made them whole. That is all you ever need to do. Just keep doing that."

Wow, Malcolm and now Tsui. I was beginning to think I was the dumbest person in the room. We walked over to Suri, who held a bottle of champagne in one hand, the other clutching O's. I kneeled down, so we were at eye height.

"Suri, my love, I must apologize to you and to Tsui. I asked him to come with me so you could hear what I had to say, and I hope you forgive me, lass, for my stupidity."

Tsui joined me down on one knee in front of Suri. I could feel strength and understanding coming off him in waves and suddenly felt a kinship to the man. "Suri, Tsui, I apologize for my outburst earlier. I ask for your forgiveness, as it was completely inappropriate."

"Of course, Laughlin. I hold no grudge in the least, your apology's accepted."

One down, and one to go.

"Suri, lass, I love you and hope that I can redeem myself in your eyes. Please tell me what I can do to make this right."

Suri released O's hand and handed Mo the bottle of champagne. "You just did, Laughlin, thank you."

I pulled her onto my knee and kept her balanced while I laid a deep, passionate kiss on her raspberry-painted lips. When I pulled back, I said, "Let's get this party started."

"That's my cue," Montana shared a mischievous smile, "and I have a surprise." She took the bottle up to the small stage with her and grabbed the microphone. "I want to congratulate the happy couple. I believe their life will be filled with as much love and adventure as Adam and I share."

There was laughter from Declan and Geoff, who, of course, knew the couple very well. "Okay, hopefully not as much adventure as Adam and I have had." More chuckling. "I was shocked to learn that Suri had her head buried so deep in the yoga world that she had never heard of my band."

I looked at Suri, who was smiling up at Montana. "So, I decided to bring my band to her, to play for her special day."

My eyes hadn't moved from Suri's face, so I was the first to see the expression of happy shock play over her features.

"Suri, Laughlin, here to perform for your pleasure is *Behind Blue Eyes*."

Suri jumped off my knee and started clapping enthusiastically, like a kid at a concert.

I watched as two men came from another doorway. The one carrying a guitar looked a lot like Montana and must have been her twin. She moved to the drum kit while he took the microphone from her.

"It's been a while since I was here. Nothing like Scotland to get the blood moving." He looked at Suri and me. "Congratulations, Mr. and Mrs. Campbell, this one is for you." The band played a rocking tune that immediately had everyone in the room dancing. Suri was so happy, she had a permanent grin pasted on her face.

Their next song was our dance, and Montana sang some haunting Gaelic song that sent shivers up my spine. Suri's energy changed, and she almost floated as I held her. She was so present with me, so surreal that everyone else in the room disappeared.

Next up was *Leave the Door Open*, and the floor around us filled with a few dancing couples—Declan and Skyla, Malcolm had Octavia, Marcus and Lenore. The song didn't require drums, so Montana grabbed Adam.

Next up was a *Behind Blue Eyes*' original that had us sweating and in need of slowing down, and then came one last song before it was time to slow down and eat, the new *Beautiful Mistakes*, by Maroon 5 & Megan Thee Stallion. Suri took Sir Henry for a spin as he hadn't danced yet. Octavia asked Ace, who tried to refuse, but she coaxed him up. Montana took Geoff, and Lenore grabbed Dan. Glancing at Marcus, I could see him stewing silently in rage. I wanted to laugh, as Dan was happily married and posed no threat to Marcus' current obsession, Lenore.

I watched as Suri chose Tsui next and they moved around the floor like they were floating. Those yogis had something special. Montana switched to Declan, and the two were laughing and joking while they danced. Skyla asked me to dance, and I accepted. From across the room, Suri beamed at us. She had no issues, and I suddenly felt a weight removed. I had to remind myself to have fun, that these people were not the bad guys. These were my friends, new and old, and it was time to act like it.

I swung Skyla around the floor as she giggled, very similarly to my new wife. I kept up a bevy of humor and found myself having as much fun as she appeared to be. Then, Mrs. C and Sir Henry came onto the floor. I think everyone in the room's breath caught. Sir Henry, I knew, had been lonely since the passing of his wife, and these two adults were both in their late fifties, way too young to pack it in and give up on second chances.

Sir Henry moved gracefully with an old-world charm that was usually only seen at the few social gatherings held by Scottish nobility's upper echelons. He seemed to be keeping Declan's mother entertained while he swept her around the room. I glanced at the giant Scot, whose expression was unreadable as he watched his mother, while his dance partner smirked with a knowing smile.

When the song came to an end, Sir Henry bowed and kissed the back of Mrs. C's hand, and she did a curtsy to the loud applause from the rest of us. Blushing, she hurried from the room with the excuse to check on dinner.

A few minutes later, we were called to the dining room, and I was seated between my new wife, on my left, and Ace Standford, on my right. Montana was across from us and watched us speculatively out of the corner of her eye while she spoke animatedly with Skyla and Declan.

"Ace, finally a moment to talk. How was the flight?"

"Luxurious as it always is. Everything my brother-in-law does is top shelf, just like his whiskey."

"Yes, Adam is quite a man, hard to believe he is real at times, eh, the way he can look you in the eyes."

Ace cracked a smile. "The soul-searching artist. Yeah, I wonder what it's like in his head sometimes."

"Busy, I would imagine, with being married to spritely Montana."

Now he chuckled. He was warming up to me, which was exactly what I wanted. "Yes, she is… something. You'd think marriage and having children would have calmed her down, but not in the least. The best thing Adam ever did was convince Declan to work for the twins so he could catch a break." Now we were getting somewhere exciting, and like the expert guide I was, I moved the conversation to his family and his parents without him being the slightest bit wiser as to my intentions.

"Montana mentioned your father died in an explosion. That is not only tragic but highly unusual, isn't it? How many casualties were there, other than your father?"

Ace seemed like a statue, and I wondered if he was going to answer me. "He was the only casualty, and yes, I have learned that is unusual based on where the explosion occurred."

"So, it's been investigated then?"

"Yes."

"But you are not satisfied with the results?"

The big man beside me glanced at me with a glimmer of curiosity. "Until recently, it was dead and buried, but yes, I am curious and find it all rather strange."

"I do as well. Many strange events are happening in what appears to be sporadic and disjointed ways, but I highly doubt that is the case. Like Declan's buddy being kidnapped, and still, nothing has been heard from his friend. My half-brother, Malcolm, his mother, who is currently a guest of the Glasgow

Psychiatric clinic, had my father killed. At least I think she did. Once I'm finished with this wedding and Geoff and I have talked with a few others, it will be time for me to dig into that particular mystery. It just seems like when anyone gets too close to knowing someone in the Templars or has Templar knowledge, they vanish. I feel there is a holding place somewhere, and all of our friends and family are being kept there." I dropped the nugget, what I had been feeling but hadn't voiced, that maybe they were not dead, but perhaps being held.

Ace looked at me as if trying to decipher my meaning. "I wish you luck." He turned back to his food. Wait, that wasn't supposed to happen.

"Ace, if your father is alive, wouldn't you want to know about it?"

"Who are you, Laughlin, that you think you can find the answers when even Geoff hasn't been able to?"

"That is a good question. For one, I have someone in custody who knows more than they are saying. For two, that man, Tsui, is the son of the grandmaster himself. It doesn't go higher, and lastly, I want to know as much as you do. I'm not sure what Geoff's motivations are."

I said it, threw myself out to the wind trying one of Suri's tactics, and prayed it didn't backfire.

Ace Stanford gave me the first genuine smile I'd seen and said, "I'm in."

Music to my ears. "Good, then we will talk more later. I think I have kept you to myself long enough, Mr. Stanford. And thank you for attending, for I truly wanted to make your acquaintance."

Ace grinned again. "Understood." Then he turned to his younger brother on his right, and our moment ended.

Chapter 11

Octavia

There were all kinds of weird happenings at this gathering. From what information I could garner, Laughlin, Geoff, and Marcus were part of the Knights Templar, known as the Masons. Adam and Declan were also a part, but to what extent, I did not know. And the biggest shock of all was Tsui Tran was also a player, known as Sir William Rothley, the missing heir to the Rothley seat in Leicestershire

This information, or rather the players, all had secondary motives to being here, and I could feel the energy permeating through the castle. I wondered what I had landed myself into? Suri must also be noticing all the male testosterone. I glanced at her, and she seemed to be happily seated on Laughlin's knee as he fed her tiny morsels of dinner.

It was romantic and the way he did it, so erotic. I was almost envious of what I was witnessing.

"Would you like me to feed you, O, hmm? Would you like to pretend at being a little and let Daddy feed you?" All this was husked into my ear for my hearing only. I wasn't sure what a little was, but he made it sound sexy. My lady parts squeezed in response to the picture it was painting in my imagination.

"I uh, don't know what a little is, but I can imagine. As sexy as you make it sound, I don't wish to do anything to draw the attention away from Suri, whose special day it is."

"So you think it sounds sexy when I tell you I will treat you as a little girl by feeding you, washing you? Putting you to bed, maybe with a bad girl, or perhaps even a good girl spanking, is hot? Dually noted, my dear.

"I turned large eyes on him. "What? That is what you meant? I take it back."

Malcolm's smile was more predatory than I'd yet witnessed. "You see, O, it's not what your brain chose, but what your body chose."

"I hate to disagree with you, Malcolm, but I believe it was your sexy voice and not what you said."

His smile changed to one of congenial friendliness. "Right, makes total sense." He dropped the topic with such speed, I felt a loss, like my natural ability to explore conceptually was taken away. With the moment over, I couldn't help wondering if he was right. Would what he referred to be stimulating?

I gazed at the array of people at the table and wondered what secret proclivities they engaged in. My eyes strayed to Tsui. He'd been one of my closest friends for the past nine years. The closest until I met Suri, yet he was filled with so many secrets. Did I really know him, or maybe all relationships were what Malcolm had said to me in the forest, energy connections. Did it really matter what Tsui's non-yogi name was? I was born Stacey, Suri was born Mary. We had adopted aspects of ourselves that our birth names and early selves could not contain, so did that mean we had secrets?

When our meal ended half an hour later, I was still deep in thought, processing my observations. I hadn't done that since before I left New York, and although that was only a few days ago, I felt like it was an entire person ago. I was different now and changing rapidly. Rapid growth was upon me in ways I had dreamed about back in the studio but which had been elusive. I now realized that one could only grow so much inside their chrysalis. At some point, the butterfly needed to break free.

Chapter 12

Laughlin

It was time to meet with Adam, Ace, Marcus, and Tsui. Needing distractions for the other guests, Montana offered to take the ladies to the lagoon and a stone effigy out in the fields a mile or two beyond the castle. Declan and Eddy went along to accompany them for safety and talk about the land's history.

The remaining men were going golfing at the Royal Troon, the most famous course in the world. The bets were laid as the men paired off into teams. My brother had managed to get Alex as his teammate. I was told that he was a fantastic golfer and knew my brother had picked him on purpose.

I began with, "Okay, gentlemen, what I am about to share, only two other people know about, Declan and my wife, as they discovered it. I've been working to uncover the secret of the clan connections between my family. As we have discovered, Suri has been kept in the dark as to her Templar heritage. It is up to us to determine the long game and who is responsible. As Tsui is entirely unrelated but is the highest on the Templar scale that one can aspire to, I have asked him to join us, as he may be able to shed light on our discoveries. Follow me."

The three of us followed Adam as he led us to a tapestry that hung in the hallway close to the kitchen and dining room. A tapestry I must have passed a good dozen times already. He pulled it back and opened a hidden door. Handing us flashlights, he then closed the door. We were immediately plunged into total darkness.

"Adam, is this part of the original castle?"

"Yes, and no, these escape routes were created and expanded on so many times, it's hard to know what is original or part of the original expansion done about two hundred years ago. But where we are headed is to the bowels of the castle."

I was about to ask a question when Tsui spoke. "This land was under constant warfare, and I believe if you follow this, it snakes through the dungeons and out the back somewhere and connects with the hillside about a mile yonder."

Our flashlights now on, we glanced at Tsui in surprise. "My early education was Templar lore, and this castle, although no longer listed in any public reference, had more Templar action than Roswell or Sinclair land."

I shuffled on the landing, overtly watching Tsui. The man was here for a reason. The wedding was a cover for him to be here. "Tsui, you said you grew up with Templar lore, but you have been missing for over a decade. What happened?" It was an eery feeling, standing in the enclosed recesses of the old castle with only our flashlights. The entire vibe reminded me of an old Vincent Price movie.

"I had to go into hiding after a SOG assassin shot me one night just after I graduated from high school."

So he, too, had been or was a target. "Aren't you worried about being here with so many high-profile Templars?"

Tsui smiled, and in the lighting, it looked sinister. "Do I look worried to you?"

"It's time to continue, gentlemen, follow me," Adam beckoned.

The conversation halted as we moved down two levels and past the old dungeons. I tried to imagine what it would have been like to be held captive in such a lightless space. Pure hell, I imagined, and then, of course, there was the torture, the cold, and lack of food. I would be surprised to learn if anyone survived more than a month in this dank horror.

We continued following Adam down to the end of the room and passed the door that Tsui had remarked on, although he had never been here before. There was a pantry ahead and what looked like a dead end. Adam moved a sack of grain and then pressed a panel on the wall that had been hidden behind it.

A wall opened, and with it, the smell of water. "If you're wondering what that smell is, Declan has informed me that we are going deep below the surface, and these last two levels of tunnels are beneath the water."

"Actually, this castle had a moat around it five hundred years ago. It stands to reason that the water would still be here," Tsui commented casually. The man was too well informed for my comfort.

"Then you know that this castle is just but the fifth genera-tion of what was originally a Roman fort," Adam said from the front of the line. Down where we were, we had to walk single file.

"But did you know that it is an extension of the Antonine Wall? Hidden from the books and unknown to any but Templars."

We stopped walking and turned to look at Tsui, who was

at the rear of our line as we made our way through the narrow tunnel.

"That can't be. I've looked and found nothing that connects this land, albeit as close as it is to Falkirk. It stands to reason, but nothing I've seen points to this being a roman fort location." Adam seemed shocked.

"There is more. You will know of William Wallace, of course. His greatest and closest companion was Sir John Graham, or Sir John De Graeme. He was a Templar Knight; did you know that? When William left Scotland to gain an education, he went to France and into the home of the De Graemes, where he received an education.

I believe William Wallace was trained in Templar fighting skills and strategies. I also believe that these tunnels ultimately lead to De Graeme's ancestral property. Somewhere in a forty-minute, underground walk from this castle, I believe lies the greatest uncovered treasure in history."

"Holy shit," I uttered for lack of a better term. While hard to see as there were two bodies ahead of me and we were still walking in limited lighting provided by our flashlights, Adam looked genuinely shocked, which was saying something, as the artist's expressions were usually cool and relaxed. I'd never seen that look on his face before.

But Tsui wasn't done with us yet. "Don't you find it odd, gentlemen, that Sir Henry, a long-time known friend of the De Graemes, took in the illegitimate son of his best friend? And became a confidant of yours, Laughlin, and now he seems awfully cozy with Geoff."

No one answered this. Tsui didn't require us to, but gave us pause to think of the dynamics surrounding us.

Then Adam asked, "Does Geoff know how close this castle is to De Graeme? Is that why he brought us here all those years ago to snoop?"

"I don't know his motivations, but I can tell you he knows

much more than he is sharing with you, Adam, and as his only heir, that gives me pause. He also reached out to Laughlin about issues that seemed to follow your happy gathering. He knew about Malcolm, and he knew about Annie and your father, Laughlin, I'm sure of it. Maybe these circumstances were set in motion to bring us together and get rid of us."

Then we heard it, a slight clicking sound. "Turn around, run back, quick," Adam yelled. Tsui led, with the rest of us on his heels. Then, the explosion went off behind us, propelling us through the doorway that led up the stairs. We raced as fast as we could, catching our breaths outside the cells on the second level. Behind us, we heard the devastation of rock, water, and shifting earth.

"We'd better get out of here, just in case another bomb is set to go off."

We reached the landing and moved the tapestry back, to sunshine pouring in through the stained glass window on the hall's opposite side. No one spoke as we made our way through the castle, the quiet after the explosion lending a quality of eeriness.

When we found ourselves in a sizeable office-type room with a bar and comfortable leather lounge chairs, Ace barked, "What the hell is going on? Is this Geoff's doing?"

"Or made to look like it is," Adam said.

"Tsui, if you hadn't stopped and shared your shocking news, we'd all be dead or soon would be buried beneath the earth. Did you know?"

"I didn't, but I felt a tug that said to go no further, and I needed to formulate words I thought you would respond to, and thankfully you did. But I fear this is far from over." He gazed around the room meaningfully, and Adam turned on music as we moved in closer.

Tsui whispered, "Adam, we need to check this place for bugs. I don't trust that an insider hasn't planted them." Then he sat back and said, "That was splendid, gentlemen. I do love a good game of chess."

"And you won again, Tsui. I'm beginning to think I'm not as good a player as I once was."

We took turns talking about non-essential things and then whispering our plan. I was beginning to feel that no place was safe.

When the ladies returned, bubbling with their enthusiasm, I think we all breathed a sigh of relief that they hadn't been the target. After dinner, Adam was going to talk to Eddy and Declan outside. He needed to find out if Geoff or any of Eddy's men knew anything about bugs. We needed to find our guilty party, and we only had forty-eight hours to do it before everyone would depart for their respective homes.

Chapter 13

Malcolm

I had been away from Octavia all day, and while I enjoyed golfing. I had played on the famous golf course many times. So it came as no surprise to anyone when Alex and I won the bet.

We came back to the castle slightly inebriated from our long day of golf and drinking, and I couldn't wait to get O alone for some bed sport. I was drumming my fingers with impatience for our dinner to end so I could whisk her away when I felt eyes on me. Glancing nonchalantly around the table, I found Laughlin gazing at me intently. He blinked and then looked away, then back at me.

Odd behavior, but thinking he had something private to say, I used the bathroom as an excuse and left the dining room. Laughlin followed me down to my suite and guided us into the bathroom, turning on the water taps full blast.

"Malcolm, I will be brief, as I don't wish to raise suspicions. Listen to me, brother. While you were gone and the ladies out exploring, there was an explosion, down beneath the castle. I have a lot to fill you in on, but you need to know that we have been searching the castle since the explosion for hidden devices, and we have found a dozen already. There is bound to be one in your room, so keep your topics general, no personal history. People, connections, don't talk about them unless you are outside. If things get weird before we leave in two days, it's just a few of us shaking the branches. Don't worry, just have my back and keep your eye on O at all times, okay?"

I wanted to ask more but understood that a bathroom break could only take so long. Laughlin left, and I waited five more minutes before heading back to the dining room with two bottles of wine in hand to make it look like I had a mission other than the bathroom. After dinner, the group landed in the giant family games room where we had the wedding after-party.

I noticed Adam, Eddy, and Declan had disappeared and glanced at my father, Henry, who was in deep conversation with Geoff Northrop. There was something in the way they talked that pulled on my memory, but I couldn't place it. The longer I watched the two, the more I was sure I had met Geoff years before.

"Hey, sexy man, wanna teach me a lesson."

I reached behind me and pulled O over the back of the couch and onto my lap. "That depends. What type of lesson would you consider appropriate? Have you been a good girl or a bad girl?"

O's pupils dilated. Despite her protestations, I felt she needed to know what a little was. I had zero experience, but a college buddy said his girlfriend was a little, and he talked about her when he drank too much. I found it bizarre, yet intriguing, and with my minor in psychology, the idea of creating a set of boundaries for her to operate within to test her was exciting. I stood up with her in my arms. "Come, I think it's time for that lesson now."

O squealed with excitement as I stood. She waved goodbye to her friends, who waved back enthusiastically, all except Montana, who, of course, made a lewd comment about making babies.

I tossed O on our bed from a good six feet away and then pounced on her when she landed. "Now, little girl, it's time for your lesson." I turned her over and began spanking her ass through her leggings as she squealed and tried desperately to move away. This was a playful session—an old-fashioned cat and mouse game. O's token resistance was enough to make our game fun.

I'd let her escape a little, raising her hopes, and then pull her back and land a few more spanks on her ass. It was funny how allowing her to fight back allowed her to take harder swats. The amateur psychologist in me wondered if that was because providing distraction allowed the receiver a neurological reprieve?

It didn't take long for O's squeals to turn to wanton panting interspersed with loud moans and coy mewls. "Please, take me, Malcolm, haven't I had enough?"

"Stop squirming, and I may reward you." Immediately, she stopped squirming. I pulled her over my lap for some severe spanking, interspersing hard slaps to her backside and lighter slaps to her mons. Her pitiful, mewling need was creating a raging hard-on in my pants.

I pulled her up abruptly and stood her between my legs. "Go over to the door and turn and face me, but first, take off your clothes." O took off her clothes and walked to the door. She was seriously turned on. The junction at her thighs was wet and glistening with her essence. If I performed the right move, I could probably have her coming in three seconds.

"Drop to your knees and crawl to me." O dropped to her

knees and licked her lips as she began a sexy crawl to my feet. I was enjoying learning all the ways she would submit to me in the bedroom. "Look at me, O."

She gazed up at me with so much lust, it almost undid me. "Now say, 'please take me, Daddy'." This was the test. At least I thought it was. I really didn't know what the hell I was doing, but I wanted to see if, by calling me *Daddy*, I could take her to a new level of pleasure. I thought she would stand up and tell me to go fuck myself, but then the most beautiful thing happened.

O nudged forward, getting as close to my inner legs as possible, and gazing up at me with a look of adoration, she said the words, "Please, Daddy, please take your little girl and show her pleasure."

I don't know what got into me, but I almost lost my load. I picked her up off the floor and placed her on her knees at the edge of my bed. I widened her knees and gently slapped her opening, tapping her clit, and she lost it. O screamed out and writhed on the bed, her body wracked with a powerful orgasm.

I grabbed her hips, slid into her well-lubricated channel, and began pumping. Every several thrusts, I released one hand and slapped her clit, and she went insane, bucking and writhing, so vocally that I was worried the entire castle would hear us.

I pulled out and, using her essence, lubricated her back hole opening and slowly slid in. Once I was fully seated. I reached around and played with her clit while O alternated between howling and begging. She was so over the top in her sensations, she was barely coherent.

I began to work her ass as I played with her clit, and whenever I felt her walls start to tighten, I smacked her clit, and she tumbled over the edge. I lost count of how many orgasms she had before I unloaded inside her.

I gently pulled out, and she collapsed on the bed. I got up and cleaned up in the bathroom, bringing back fresh towels to wash her. I rolled her onto her back and spread her legs. She lay perfectly still, her eyes the barest of slits as she watched me.

I deposited the dirty laundry into the hamper and climbed on the bed, pulling her in tight to me. We lay facing the window, watching the last traces of pink disappear into twilight. "How are you feeling, O?"

"Like a wet noodle. I have never been like that before. I'm almost embarrassed."

"Embarrassed, why?" I caressed her hair, waiting for her to respond. "O?"

"Yes?"

"Answer me."

"Yes, sir. I meant to say that I felt different, completely out of my mind with lust, for starters, but beyond that, I feel like I just went traveling on a shooting star. And, well, this is going to sound so bad, so please, forgive me in advance. But when you treated me that way, I would have done anything you asked, I was so turned on."

"Now, why was that so hard to say? Hmm, what is wrong with what you shared?"

"Because I feel like I gave up my free will. And, Malcolm, I liked it."

So, my yogi, O, was a submissive, perfect. "Octavia, you should never be embarrassed about your feelings, and to be honest, I have never done anything like that with anyone before. I just went with my gut."

"Really?"

"Really. But now that I know how much you like it, we will do more play like that."

"Malcolm."

"Yeah, baby, what is it?"

"I'm falling really hard, so please don't forget your promise."

"I won't, O, don't worry, everything will be fine."

She was silent, and I was about to ask her a question when her breathing deepened. My precious woman had fallen asleep, and I wasn't far behind.

Chapter 14

Suri

I was floating in a surreal universe; my two besties and I were floating in the lagoon. This was my third day in a row, and I was determining how to ask the Northrops how often I could invade their property to use it after they left for Canada.

Whatever issue Tsui and Laughlin had was past and they now seemed to get on better than I could have hoped for. But I couldn't help feeling they shared a secret. Last night in bed, I'd planned to seduce the information out of Loc but earned myself some fun time over his knee and then between his legs, and my seduction plan went out the window along with my moans.

So now I would work on Tsui to see what he would share. Currently, he and O were splashing each other in the lagoon. I was happy that only the three of us came, although we did invite the others.

Declan had some things to do in Glasgow, and Skyla went with him instead of taking the train home. We had a tearful goodbye, but with me now living in Scotland, we had made a plan to do lunch the following week.

Adam was finally doing a tour of the town and local commerce. All the men went, except Declan and Tsui, and my sister, who said she needed some downtime and decided to stay at the castle. I moved out of the water onto a flat slab of rock and watched my two besties goof around.

When their shenanigans were over, they joined me on the slab. "Tsui, don't you find it funny that we three have new names? We're different, but we fit into this world, one that I couldn't have imagined."

Being English, you would assume that Tsui would be super pale, but years of being in Tibet and laboring outside had given him a light golden skin color, and lying now in the sun, he almost looked like a golden statue.

"What do you mean by fit, Suri? Do you mean that our evolved selves still have a place in traditional society, away from yoga?"

"Yes, precisely what I mean."

"Well, wasn't that the point? Why would you run from one place to another just to hide there? Yoga and spiritual growth are not for hiding but for personal education and growth and as a support in tough times. You were never meant to just stay there, beautiful Mary."

I hated that name. It meant sorrow, and Mary had had plenty of that. Suri, however, was built for adventure. But I was both, what I was and what I am, and maybe I hadn't combined my dark and light as well as I'd thought? But that was the point to being with Laughlin, well, besides the fact I was completely and utterly in love. He brought my pieces together, and maybe one day, I could do that on my own.

"Stop stressing, woman, you are exactly where you need to be, are you not?"

"Ugh, Tsui, stop turning the tables on me. I wanted to ask

you a question." On Tsui's other side, O had remained quiet throughout our exchange. She had her eyes closed, and it would be easy to presume she was sleeping, but I knew she was listening.

"What's going on?"

He cracked an eye open and gazed at me questioningly. "Is there more to that question, Suri, or am I supposed to guess what is on your mind?"

"When we came back yesterday, Laughlin, Ace, Adam, and you all seemed stressed. Did you learn something about the mystery?"

O rolled onto her side, propping her head upon her fist. I guess she had noticed, too, and was curious.

"I take it your men decided to keep you ignorant for a reason, so far be it for me to tell you."

O sat up and glared down at Tsui. "I don't belong to any man. I've known Malcolm for less than a week. I am my own person, thank you very much."

Tsui laughed great guffawing laughter that startled the birds in the nearby trees. "O, you are precious, but if you are truly blind, then let me help you. Malcolm is your other half, it is quite clear to us all that you are a couple, and you have submitted yourself into his care."

O sucked in a breath. "How did you know that?"

"Because, love, it is obvious, and besides, you have no game face."

Now it was my turn to laugh. Tsui was right in that O didn't have a game face.

"Tsui, please, tell me what is going on."

"There was an explosion at the castle yesterday, down in the caverns deep below, and was meant to kill the four of us, but it failed. We are still trying to determine if it is the work of an insider from our group, with our main suspects being Geoff Northrop and Henry Fitzwilliam."

Both O and I were shocked into silence. I was thinking and sending out tendrils of energy as I sought the truth of what was going on. "Do you think our wedding here was meant to happen so we would all be in the same place at the same time?"

Tsui nodded at me in approval. "I did, but that would mean that Montana or Adam were the ones who set this up, and I know it wasn't them."

I sat still and rooted myself. I became acutely aware of the sounds of nature that surrounded me. Almost hearing the bugs walking on the leaves in the trees, so tuned, was I. "Sir Henry has been here before." I talked in a low, hypnotic tone as I kept my eyes closed and used my reiki skills to seek answers. "He knows who is behind this. Geoff is walking a dangerous path. A pawn to two masters and will soon no longer be with us."

My eyes flew open at my words, and glancing at my friends, I could see their eyes wide in astonishment.

"Suri, when did you become a seer?" O asked.

"I'm not. I just do reiki, you know, to help heal people."

"Oh, you are much more than that, love. Reiki, yes, but that was way more than funneling energy. You can control how you use the energy, and you used it for sight. You are a seer, and I'm sure as you get older, even more gifts will present from your amazing abilities."

I was shocked, as I had never thought to analyze my healing gift and assumed it had come from my reiki initialization, that I was like everyone else with an ability now to hone in and help send healing vibes into people. Then I thought about that time in the hot tub with Montana. That had been more, I realized now, than simple reiki. I had seen the blackness and pulled it out of her.

"Suri, let's do an experiment. Go back to closing your eyes

and focusing. Ask if Annie, Malcolm's mother, is not who she appears to be," Tsui suggested.

I did, closing my eyes and clearing my mind of any other thoughts. I asked the question in my mind and heard a resounding *yes*. "Did you guys hear that? A voice said yes."

Both my companions shook their heads no. "I didn't hear a voice, but I knew the answer would be yes. Do you think my thought process answered yours?"

"I don't know. Let's try again, but this, Tsui, think of the color blue. That will keep your thoughts away from Malcolm's mother, and maybe my answer will change. Tell me when you're ready." I closed my eyes and waited until Tsui said "ready" and sent out my question, and again, I received the same answer, *yes*.

"Tsui, how did you do with blue?"

"Perfect, I kept my mind steady, and you?"

"I received the same answer with the same voice."

"What does it sound like?" O asked.

I could still hear the sound. It was omnipotent, not from this earth or maybe not from this realm. "Like God," I answered. Our eyes turned heavenward, and with reverence, we watched the sky as we lay back down. For the next hour, we cloud gazed and once in a while shared verbally what we were seeing. What was extraordinary was, for the first time, I could hear what they were thinking, or rather, impressions of their thoughts on what they were seeing washed over me in waves of consciousness. I felt I'd gone down the rabbit hole with Alice.

Chapter 15

Laughlin

The tour of the village had been an eye-opener. Adam showed us the new streets, the updated village school that now sported an annex and had enough children to support a complete education.

In some ways, the children going to school locally were getting a better education than some of the more prestigious private schools in the bigger cities, and I was very impressed. The language offer was beyond impressive—Gaelic Scots, Latin, British English, and the option to learn an Asian language or another European language.

There were currently several students learning German, and only two had taken on the problematic language of Mandarin. European history was a rich blend of local and all of Europe and included Canada, where many Europeans moved for many reasons over the past few hundred years.

Music was offered, and gifted students could also apply to music school on a full scholarship. This was Alex's contribution. They had an art school that offered art classes in drawing and painting and drama and dance. The buildings were built by the locals, and I could see the love that went into all that we saw.

We stopped in to visit a local silversmith who had remained in the town despite his now worldwide renown. Apparently, he had started as a weapons maker and was a school chum of Declan's. He also made the wedding bands that Adam and Montana wore. I perused his shop with great interest. His work was original and appealed to me.

Afterward, we filed into the local pub that had built a patio extension. We sat down in the sun with pints of beer and more appetizers than we could eat. Everywhere we went, people were friendly and outspoken in their appreciation for the Northrops, especially Adam, who seemed to be very hands-on with the town and knew everyone by name.

Adam's ability to connect with people so profoundly had me thinking about Roswell, a population of about two thousand, for whom I was now responsible. I knew nothing about anyone who lived in the Saint Clair lands, and I needed to. If anything, this trip had been humbling in so many ways and taught me how detached I was. It was time to change that. I was mulling over changes I could inspire and support financially.

I learned from googling that my town didn't even have a school, and children were bussed into the city or driven by their parents, who predominantly worked in the city. I had been so busy with cleaning up our oceans, I had forgotten that people and education from the ground up could save our world's future.

I was almost heady when it was time to leave the bar, from the beer and my plans. As we walked back to the castle, I found myself beside Adam. "You have no idea how much you have inspired me, Adam. This is remarkable."

He gave me one of his soul-searing looks. "Not really. It just takes planning and execution."

"I have ideas, things I would like to be a catalyst for in Roswell. Do you think you could be available for questions?"

"Of course, Laughlin, we are friends. You can ask anything, anytime." That was something I had noticed about the Canadians. They were a lot more open and giving than any other group of people I had met. I could see why most of the world liked them, despite their long line of crappy leaders.

When we arrived back, I was greeted by a flying Suri. She saw us coming and had launched herself off the front stairs into my arms, to the chuckles of my companions. "I have a place I wish to take you. I have things to share," she whispered in my ear.

My cock sprang to attention, and looking up at the sky, I saw that we had a few hours of light left. "Okay, my bratty yogi, let's go."

She squealed with excitement as I lowered her, and then, taking my hand, she began to pull me through the castle toward a back entrance where two waiting backpacks sat. "We're having a picnic dinner," she said in the way of explanation.

Together, we walked out the back of the castle and across the moorland. The energy in the air back here was completely different than where I had just been. I could almost imagine thousands of Highlanders fighting here, the ghost sounds of their swords ringing through the air.

Half an hour later, we came upon a ring of standing stones, and when we entered it, I felt that ringing I'd heard before intensified. Maybe it hadn't been my imagination. Suri laid out a blanket and then opened the second pack for our victuals.

She opened a bottle of red wine and poured it into an earthenware mug. Around us, the air was shimmering. There was no other way to say it. It was like a separate world lived within these stones. I have lived in Scotland all of my life and within feet of one of the oldest and most unique places on earth, the Roswell abbey, which had been initially erected in the first century.

Yet here I was, with my wife, in a standing stone and feeling magic all around us for the first time in my life. We sat, and Suri handed me a cup of wine. "To us," she said, holding up hers for me to cheer.

"To us," I repeated, and our mugs clinked together.

Suri giggled. "Not your typical crystal, is it?"

"No," I answered, "but it is very earthen and therefore appropriate for this place. It is something. Did Montana tell you about it?"

"No, it was Mrs. C. When we came back from the lagoon, she told me I should bring you here."

"Oh, she did, did she? And why do you suppose that is?"

Suri blushed. "Well, apparently, if you make love within the circle, you will get pregnant."

That was a shock. Was she ready to have a baby? Was I? "So by bringing me here, are you saying you are ready to have a child?"

"Would it be wrong if I said yes?"

"No, lass, not wrong, but do you feel ready to be burdened with such a large responsibility? I never thought I would be a father, and I still feel like I need to learn you, but if you are ready, then so am I."

Suri took a big gulp of wine. "I have something to tell you, Laughlin. Annie, Malcolm's mother, and Sir Henry are responsible for all of your problems, not Geoff. Although he is not entirely innocent, he has more going on than he is sharing."

I was about to ask how she knew that when I felt the earth

beneath us shift, and before I could shout out a warning, our world gave way, and we were tumbling below the ground. I didn't fall far, but I landed with a hard *thunk* on the rocks below. The screech Suri had let out with the shift in the earth was quickly silenced.

Chapter 16

Malcolm

I t was growing late, with no sign of Suri or my brother. After questioning everyone, I found out from Declan's mother that they had gone to the standing stone about half an hour away and should have been back by dark.

I found Adam with Ace and Tsui and told them the pair was missing. "We need to find them, as I can't shake the feeling that something has happened to them."

"Okay, let's keep this between us in case it has something to do with the explosion yesterday. By the way," Adam added, "Eddy is clean and was so angry, he wanted to fire all of his guys on the spot despite knowing they are loyal."

"I was about to tell you, it's not Geoff, although he is involved with some unsavory characters. It is Sir Henry," Tsui finished.

"Let's talk about this on the way. Please, we need to go and find them now."

We grabbed a rope, weapons, flashlights, and a first aid kit because we had no idea what we would find.

"Look, there he is," I called excitedly. I'd been calling to Laughlin during the entire walk to the stones and was shocked when we arrived, to find a sinkhole where the center of the ring once was. I shone my flashlight down into the sinkhole and saw an arm in the air and knew it was Laughlin. Ace, Tsui, Eddy, Adam and myself gazed down into the twenty-foot drop. "Damn good thing we brought rope. I'll go down," Tsui offered.

"No, I'll do it. I do rope climbing at the gym almost every day of the week and can scale up and down within seconds." Ace and Eddy took the rear, Tsui in front, and Adam kept the flashlight shining down while I scaled the pit.

When I landed, I saw that my brother was covered in debris and had only managed to get his arm free. "Hang on, Loc." I used my hands like shovels and uncovered him quickly and then saw he had been pinned down by a rock. Using every bit of strength I had, I managed to roll it far enough off him that he could pull himself out.

"We need to find Suri."

"Do you have any idea where she is?"

"No, but when the ground gave out, she was only a foot away from me."

"Okay, I'm sending you up, and I will find her."

"No, I'm okay. I will find my wife." I was going to argue with him but even injured, he was a bull, so I left it alone.

"Suri! Suri! Laughlin called. There was no response. "Suri! Damn it, woman, where are you?"

"I'm here, Loc, and perfectly safe. Look what I found."

Beside me, I heard my brother groan in frustration. We climbed over to where we heard Suri's voice and saw that she stood inside a cavern.

"Look!" she said excitedly. She moved inward, revealing a stone effigy.

"Adam," I yelled, "you'd better come down here.

"Is everyone okay?" Adam yelled back.

"Yes, but I think we just discovered that tunnel you mentioned on our walk." We heard dirt and debris shift, and then Adam was beside us, adding his light to mine and giving us a better view of what lay inside.

"This is the tunnel. It's been right under us all this time," Adam commented.

"That looks like a Templar tomb," Laughlin said, moving closer. "Holy shit, that is Henry St. Clair. What is he doing here?"

"Who is Henry St. Clair?" Suri asked, her eyes huge as she took in the crypt.

"He is the son of Hugues de Payens and your ancestor, Suri. What are the Sinclairs doing here?"

"Guarding a treasure, perhaps," Adam answered.

"What do we do?" Suri queried. "Open it?"

All eyes turned to Tsui, the grandmaster's son.

"We need to protect whatever is inside. I say we set up security for tonight and come back when there is daylight, to excavate properly." Then Tsui shone his light upward, checking out the walls of the opening. "This is a junction; there is more behind that wall and," he shone his light the other way, "a little more that way as well."

"Could this be a message, Tsui, that the Sinclairs are the key?"

Even in the darkness, Tsui's blue eyes shone like gems. "Yes, the Sinclairs are definitely a key and I think it's time to talk with Suri's father. Is there a chance your sister is here as a spy, Suri?"

Suri's moss green eyes rounded in surprise. "Anything is possible, I guess. But I doubt it. If this has anything to do with my family, who else would know?"

All eyes turned my way. "What are you looking at me for?

You know I didn't know anything about this stuff until Laughlin and I met."

"Yes, that is true, but it's not you. There is a missing piece to all of this. Suri, you said you met Geoff a few years ago at a benefit in Boston for your company?"

"Yes."

"And who else was there?"

"A lot of people, it was a gala."

"Suri," Tsui broke in, "close your eyes, breathe, and visualize Geoff. He said he was friends with Stanhope senior. Did you see them together?"

"Yes."

"Who else was with them?" Tsui asked.

"Uh, his back is turned; wait, there are two men." Her eyes flew open. "Oh my god, it was my father and a man who looked a lot like you, Tsui, but older. Could it be your father?"

Leaving her question unanswered, Tsui said, "Let's get out of this pit and have Eddy get security out here stat. We need this quietly covered up. Laughlin, Suri, you two were out for a walk after dusk, got lost, and end up falling down a ravine. If anyone asks about the stones, just say you stopped and ate there and carried on. Everyone clear? Let's get out of here."

We called up that we were ready to get out of the pit. No answer came, but one at a time, we were pulled out. Imagine my surprise when I crawled over the lip of the pit to find our entire group on their knees with their hands behind their heads. Geoff, three other men, and my mother were there, holding guns on them.

"Hello, laddie," Annie said with not a whit of the psychosis she exhibited at my brother's a week earlier.

Before I could answer, Tsui spoke up. "Father, I'm surprised to see you out and about, doing your own dirty work."

"It's not what you think, William."

"Oh, sure it is," Annie cackled. "It is exactly what you think. We are going to wipe out you little upstarters and bury what's down there in a new location. Thanks for doing all the dirty work for us, boys, and lady," she said, turning her eyes on Suri.

"What did you do to my parents?" Ace asked, directing his question to the group with the guns. "Did you kill them?"

"Well, they were a complete nuisance, not wanting to share the family history and all that." Annie's eyes positively gleamed with malice.

Finally, Adam spoke, his eyes betraying his hurt and confusion. "Dad, what the hell is going on, and why are you pointing a gun at your family and friends?"

"It's not what you think, son."

"Isn't that a common theme?" Laughlin grunted.

"This has been lovely, but I have a flight to catch. Someone needs to run my massive company." Edward Stanhope glared down at Suri.

"You can't be serious," I said when I found my voice at last. "You're going to kill all of us? To what end, what is so important about what's down there that you guys would cover up the deaths of so many prominent people?"

"What's down there, Malcolm, is a treasure beyond your reckoning, a treasure our little group has been hunting for thirty years, and you kids finally brought it to us," Geoff answered. "Say your goodbyes, for life is about to end. I'm sorry, son, if there had been another way, I would have taken it."

The group of five held up their guns and pointed to our group. As I was about to die, my thoughts strayed to O. I prayed fervently that she would move on and enjoy her life. I glanced beside me at Laughlin. "Goodbye, brother, see you again someday, I hope."

The guns cocked and then gunfire rang out into the quiet of the Scottish moors.

Chapter 17

Octavia

I had been unable to locate Malcolm or Suri and wondered where they'd gone. I tried both of their cell phones, growing a little frantic when there was no answer. Malcolm had been looking for Laughlin and Suri earlier and must have still been looking.

Finally, I found Dan and Alex in the music room, with Alex's fellow bandmate, Otter. "Hey, you guys haven't seen your brother or Adam, have you? I can't find them, or Malcolm, or Laughlin. Have you?"

Alex sat very still as if he was listening to something, and then he said, "Adam, Eddy, Ace, and Tsui went looking out on the moor for your girlfriend and her husband." He was still again and then looked at Dan, his expression speaking a language I did not know either of them well enough to comprehend.

"Let's go," Dan said, "and grab some flashlights." I followed the men around as they grabbed items before heading out the back door of the castle. Montana seemed to appear out of nowhere and joined us.

"What's going on?" I whispered for her ears alone.

"Mrs. C said not long after the group left to look for Laughlin and Suri, Geoff and Henry left secretly through a tunnel. She didn't get a good feeling about it, and with Adam's suspicions, I felt we should go looking too."

I noticed then that Montana was carrying a large bow on her back with a quiver of arrows. "You're expecting trouble?"

"It never hurts to be prepared, O. Do you know any self defense, or have you trained with weapons?"

"Well, in Australia, I used a bow at camp every summer, but nothing so official as self defense training."

"But you can hit a target?"

"I can, yes."

"Good, if I go down, then use my bow." Suri had told me about her adventure in the Hebrides with Montana, and I felt better knowing she was with us. Apparently, when her family and friends had been held against their will in the very castle we were staying in for the wedding, she and Declan had freed everyone and dismantled twenty assassins. Montana was badass.

We had been walking for about fifteen or twenty minutes when we heard gunshots. We took off at a run, trying not to trip in the dark as we made our way to the stones. I was praying to every god who would listen to spare my friends' lives.

When we arrived, it was to find Geoff Northrop untying Eddy and Ace. "What the hell is going on?" Montana roared, pointing an arrow at Geoff.

"Calm down, Montana. I will explain everything in a moment."

"Don't you tell me to calm down, old man. You've been

skulking around the castle since we arrived back on the mainland, and I want to know why."

"Montana, it's okay. He's on our side," Adam's calm voice rang out in the night air.

I saw Malcolm and ran into his arms as he rose from the dirt. Laughlin, beside him and covered in dirt, helped Suri to stand up.

"What the bloody hell happened to my standing stones?"

Ace walked over and wrapped his arm around her. "It's quite a story, sis. Let's go back and have hot chocolate and we can fill you in." She looked up at her brother and nodded her head, momentarily appeased.

"Who are these people on the ground? Are they dead?" Someone had to ask; it might as well be me.

"No, wounded, but some of them may not make it. We have quite the collection of bad guys, O. Tsui's father, Sir William Rothley, Edward Stanhope the II, Cecil de Sinclair, Suri's father, Annie Smith, and Henry Fitzwilliam.

Eddy was on his phone, having a chopper brought in from Glasgow University Hospital.

Malcolm moved to Henry's side. "Why, why did you side with them, to what end?"

"Is Annie dead?"

Malcolm nodded.

"We have been in a tangled web. Annie was not a Smith, and you won't find records to the contrary. Annie was a descendant of St. Clair. She is a Sinclair and a descendant from one of the several branches who had a piece of the land that ultimately became Laughlin's grandfather's. He didn't come by it honestly."

Laughlin joined us at Sir Henry's side.

"I'm sorry, my boy," Henry said, looking up at Laughlin. "Annie Sinclair is a cousin of yours, Loc, and she has been moving the chess pieces since your father hired her. She has so much dirt on us all that we couldn't afford to let her mouth run free. We couldn't take her out, because the information would be passed along. But with all of us dead, I imagine it will all come to nothing now. Lord Rothley was her accomplice, as he figured out years ago where the treasure must be, and the two of them have been working their plan ever since."

Henry gasped and then coughed up blood. Malcolm rolled him onto his side. "Don't talk, Da. I can hear the chopper, it's almost here, just hang in."

"Laughlin, Malcolm, I love you both. Please promise to take care of each other, and when you uncover the treasure, share it with the world, or hide it again. The choice is yours." Henry took his last breath, his hand resting on top of Malcolm's.

When the chopper landed, the only one still alive was William Rothley. When the evac chopper left, Eddy went with it, so he could talk to the authorities. As the sounds of the engine disappeared, our little group was left in utter silence. Looking around the group, those who had been on their knees appeared haunted, and someone needed to take charge and get everyone home. I decided that someone was me.

"Who has a cell phone?"

"Me," Montana answered.

"Can I borrow it please?"

She handed it over, and I quickly called the castle. "Mrs. C, there have been some events. We're all okay, but we are going to need something fortifying. Can you send Thorsten out with the all-terrain? We're by the stones."

She clucked her tongue, already giving herself instructions before I'd hung up the phone. A few minutes later, the vehicle arrived with Thor in the driver's seat. He took one look around and then gathered us together like little chicks, getting us inside and driving back. He took us right to the door and helped me get everyone inside. Mrs. C took one look at the group and directed us to the family room.

She poured us hot tea and whiskey and had blankets at the ready. Then she sat down and waited with the rest of us for the only person who knew everything to finally tell us the story of what had gone down.

Chapter 18

Geoff

I would have to tell them everything, as I knew they would accept no less. I hoped that when I finished my story, my son didn't disown me. Fifteen minutes after arriving back at the castle, Adam told me to begin.

"First, I want to express that I couldn't tell any of you the truth until the drama had played itself out. Sir Henry and I, well, we spent many hours driving the conspiracy here so we could remove the players once and for all, and by players, I don't mean you, but those who held you at gunpoint."

"Please start at the beginning. I, for one, need a straight accounting of events before I can rest and do my part in cleaning up this mess," Laughlin said.

"I understand, Laughlin, and will do my best. Our story begins with my father and England. Adam, as you know, I was born in England, but I never told you my real last name, as my father had it changed after his father went missing. We are a long line of Templars, as you know, but Northrop is a bastardized version of Neuham. I was born in a village of approximately five hundred people. Still, today, it houses a great Templar church, and ceremonies are held there. When I moved your mother and myself to Canada, I erased my Templar connections and changed our name legally to Northrop. I was a young man when we came to Canada, only nineteen, and your mother, Adam, was already pregnant with you. I started from nothing and cut all ties with my family, hoping to ensure our anonymity. But about ten years ago, all of that changed, when a young artist student fell in love with a McGregor descendant."

I looked around the room and was, not for the first time, shocked by the chains of connections between the people in the room. Every one of them could draw a line between our families.

"I was approached at a worksite one day, by William Rothley Sr., Tsui's grandfather, already an old gentleman. He told me about the Templars in Scotland and about this castle. When I needed to get Montana's family and friends into hiding, I reached out to Tsui's grandfather, who has since passed." I looked at Tsui meaningfully. He understood my communication, another victim of the order wanting the treasure.

"Anyway, he had just passed the grandmastership on to his son and I believe it was only weeks later, there was an attempt on your life, Tsui, is that correct?" He nodded in affirmation. "So here is the background. Adam. Your friend Katya, who founded the gang that went after us, was funded by SOG. They have been our enemy from the beginning. Katya was sent in to woo Dan and get an invite into the McGregor/Stanford home for recognisance."

The shocked faces were confirmation that none of them knew anything about what I'd learned. "To confirm, I didn't know that until long afterward. Then Synchronicity hit and Ralph Masters was killed. That was not part of the Templars,

Montana. That was completely unrelated but happened, thus removing Katya from your home and spoiling the plans of the Templars. However, my housekeeper, whom we spoke about in the hebrideas, was also affiliated through her family with SOG, so we can assume that with Montana out of the way, the last female in the line would be dead."

"Jesus Christ," Ace uttered. "Before you go on, Geoff, is there a significance to being of the female line and not the men's?"

"There is, and it will come out as I move along. But we all know that attempts to rid the world of the tenacious Montana have failed repeatedly. So even though the Templars owned the castle under a dummy company, I coaxed them into selling it to Adam so it would remain in our hands."

"Why?" Adam asked, sitting forward, his entire being showing for the first time the stress he must have been feeling all evening.

"Because, son, if they went after you or Montana, I wanted leverage against them, and owning the place where their precious treasure was hidden seemed a good way to do it. Now we move into where Laughlin and Malcolm's stories come in. When I was first approached by Rothley Sr., he told me he and a partner in Scotland were working undercover to get secret information. Someone who had direct contact with the Sinclair heir. Of course, we now know that was Annie, but I had no idea at the time. For years, I did nothing to find out who the spy was, and I was busy removing and burying history in the hopes of keeping Templar connections from my family. Then about a year ago, I got wind that a sweep was being performed to remove the players. They either joined us or were going to be executed. When the news came down about your father, Laughlin, I knew the spy had to be in your household, and I reached out to you."

"So you were with them?"

"They certainly thought so. I have been playing the long game for years, in an attempt to learn the identities of all the major players and have them arrested. Annie and William are responsible for hundreds of deaths and missing persons."

"What about my dad? Was he also a victim?" Ace asked in a voice laced with sadness and anger.

"He was, but again, at the time I didn't know that he, too, had been approached. He worked away from home for a reason, trying to keep his kids safe, and it was your mother who was the key. After they killed your mother, in an attempt to force your father into siding with them and sharing the families heretical secrets, he took measures to ensure your safety. He had dirt on William, your father, Tsui, and was going to use it if anything happened to anyone, and for years you were left alone. Until SOG got desperate. Anyway, when we connected and Suri went missing, again, a serendipitous situation, I told Sir Henry, who was already in the know, as Annie had been using him to inform on your father, for years, Laughlin. In more recent times, on you and Suri as well."

Laughlin's face could have been carved from stone with the way he looked at me. Out of everyone in the room, Laughlin held the trophy on the deadpan stare.

"Here is the key to this all… I was told that these senior Templars had gone against the order and joined SOG. And that, too, was a lie. I found out yesterday that they had tricked SOG and used their resources for the Hebrides attack and also in Turkey and Greece, to throw you off the scent. That trip, by the way, was created by the group. Your yoga friend Tino is a soldier of the SOG and has since been removed. We can assume he has been assassinated."

I heard a gasped intake of breath from Octavia, who would have known the yogi longer than anyone in the room.

"He was sent on purpose to your studio, O, when Mary's father shared her new identity with the senior group. After

Edward was removed, there was no choice but to go after Mary next."

Everyone glanced at Suri, who was looking startled, a perfect deer in the headlights response.

"You see, Suri, you are the heir to both Stanhope and de Sinclair crowns, except, because you married Laughlin, you have effectively closed the door on the two great Sinclair branches and brought them together into one. Now, only your children can claim the title."

Poor Suri looked about ready to faint.

"They were gunning for you next, Laughlin, and they would have used Malcolm as a puppet if they could. Annie was very specific about him not being harmed, at least until he sided with you. Then she wanted him dead as well."

"Montana and Adam had joined, closing the door on the Campbell/Neuham inheritance, and only their children inherit the title. Their boys have been at risk since their birth. So in answer to your earlier question, Ace, the girls inherit from their mothers and the boys inherit from the fathers. Suri is a unique case because her first husband was an only child and is dead, and in her family, she is inheriting from her father because there is no son. But in Montana's case, it would have ended with her because she was the only girl born into a family of boys. I have been putting the pieces together for years, and if any of you had found out what I was doing, you would have assumed I was one of the bad guys. That is why I kept my knowledge secret."

"Geoff, what about Alastair Sinclair, the guy who led the attack in the Hebrides? Is he part of all of this?"

"He was part of SOG, and working under William's directive, he, too, has been terminated by Annie and William. Anyone they borrowed from SOG is dead."

"So, what now? We have Tsui. Is he to replace his father as

supreme head of this crazy mason group or go back to his old life? How does this work?" Adam asked.

"A lot of that depends on you all. We now have the keys to the mystery, a mystery that people have been trying to figure out for a thousand years. It is literally in our backyard. If you decide to keep it secret, then we need a new network to protect it. If we decide to give it up, the world will fight for a while about where the treasure belongs, and it is not just treasure, but the entire banking history of the Templars. Kings, queens, and countries owed them for a reason. I don't know if the world is ready to uncover the secrets of such a rich and bloody history."

"So our Mason thugs were hoping for what, to create chaos?" Malcolm asked.

"No, Malcolm, our Mason thugs, as you call them, were planning on using the information and the treasure to take over the world's banking system."

A collective sigh of shock rang out around the room.

"I don't understand half of this, but it sounds like we have a responsibility to the world and our ancestors. I, for one, feel that hiding this is what we should do," Suri said.

"That is a good point, but I think we should sleep on this. Eddy and Thor have secured the site, and for right now, no one beyond this room is aware of the treasure being here between our land and Sinclairs'. We have time to decide what is right and what we can live with."

Laughlin stood. "Suri and I need to clean up. I say, let's convene tomorrow before noon with our thoughts and choices on the matter. So. To be clear, this really comes down to Suri, Tsui, myself, Montana, and Adam?"

"Yes, you two couples and Tsui are the hereditary holders of the seats. and therefore, the final decision will be yours."

"Understood. Suri, come, let's go get you cleaned up. Until tomorrow, we bid you adieu."

Tsui stood next, and whatever his thoughts to what he heard were, I couldn't tell. Then everyone was up and saying goodnight and I was left to ponder the outcome, hoping that the five would make a decision that would leave the world as it was.

I'd seen the devastation the treasure hunt had created and didn't wish to see it again. I rose to my feet, feeling my age for the first time, and was glad the nightmare was now in younger, more capable hands than mine had ever been.

Chapter 19

Octavia

I didn't pretend to know half of what was talked about, but I could see the impact on Malcolm in the morning light. He had tossed and turned all night, mumbling in his sleep. Being held at gunpoint and then finding out his mother had been the criminal mastermind had been a massive jolt.

When we had finally gone to sleep, he had pulled me in tight, like I was his lifeline. It was the first time that I remember a man being vulnerable with me, trusting me. Malcolm was staring at the ceiling, and the light streaming through the windows highlighted his beautiful ruggedness.

"I'll be right back, Malcolm. Stay here, okay?" He turned his head and watched me throw on a robe and slippers and leave. I came back fifteen minutes later with a breakfast tray. He sat up in bed and fluffed out the pillows. I handed him the tray and got back in bed beside him.

"Breakfast in bed, how novel." He smiled at me, his happiness not quite reaching his eyes.

"Malcolm, is there anything I can do for you? Can I help?"

He sighed as he poured us each a cup of coffee. "I don't know what to tell you, O. I'm fine, but I'm not. I feel like I shouldn't be here, that I'm a fake. Look at where I come from. I am the product of a liaison between a cold lord and a crazy Templar assassin posing as a maid. What the hell does that make me?"

I understood where he was coming from and why he would think these things, but they weren't the truth. The truth was we are unique beings with our own divinity, and he was being pulled into a thought process that aligned him with things outside his control.

"Malcolm, I understand, but you are looking at this all wrong."

"Oh? How so?"

"The people who birthed you created a unique human being. Your DNA is unique, and only you get to write the pages of who you are. Not your history, and certainly not your birth parents. Your brother loves you, and I think he is feeling the same way. Everything he's known has been turned upside down. You two can be there for each other in ways no one else could."

He smiled, and this time it reached his cobalt eyes. "Thank you, O, that helps. Is it time to meet up and decide what to do? I don't really have a say, mind you, but I am curious as to how it will be decided on."

"Me, too, but we still have an hour until we meet. I ran into Marcus in the kitchen. Laughlin brought him up to speed this morning, and he will be there as well, being he is part of the hierarchy."

We ate in silence for a spell, then Malcolm got out of bed to put our tray on the dresser, and I got to examine his perfect body. Every bit of him was fit and trim, with long, muscular limbs. I had a sudden image of the same body, the same man, but years ahead. Still fit and trim, but with gentle aging to his posture and grey highlights running through his hair. I saw the future Malcolm, a glimpse at least. That was my message, what I'd been waiting for. I would not have been given this vision if I was not supposed to be part of it.

When he turned around and saw my expression, his became one of concern. "What is it, O, are you okay?"

"I'm better than okay, you giant Scotsman. So, tomorrow, what are our plans?"

He joined me back in bed, giving me a questioning look. "Tomorrow, we check out, and after that, we had not discussed."

I thought back to a few days before, to our time in the woods, when I saw the energy in the air, the life force of everything around us, and when I'd gazed at Malcolm, his life force was blue with a white ring around it. He'd been right about our connection. We were meant to be. I was not a creature molded by fear, not anymore. I had the power to share what I wanted, and now was that time.

"After we check out of this Shangri-La , I would like to go home with you, but under a few conditions."

Malcolm's eyes darkened to black orbs, making me shudder with excitement. "Be careful, lass, I make the conditions. I thought I made that clear."

I wasn't sure where to go with that. I chewed my lip thoughtfully as I considered his simple statement. When I saw my manipulation for what it was, trying to cover my ass out of fear, I burst out laughing. I laughed so hard that tears were leaking from the corners of my eyes. Malcolm, smiling, but not privy to my private joke, watched me, slightly bewildered. When I calmed down enough to speak, I said simply, "Okay."

I didn't have to say anything else, as he totally got it. Leaning over me, he kissed me deeply. "No need to fret, lass. I will make sure you see the world."

Feeling completely at ease with my choice, I nodded and returned the kiss. It wasn't hungry or desperate but held a promise of things to come—a future for him and me that I didn't need to worry about.

We entered the ballroom right on time and found that everyone from last night was there, and Lenore and Marcus had been added to the group.

"Thank you all for being on time. I have added Sir Marcus and Suri's sister, Lenore, to our little group and have filled them in on the basics. I would ask that Tsui, as the highest-ranking among us, take over at this time."

Tsui nodded his head and stood up. My friend was not the same man he'd been only a few days earlier. When I met Tsui, he had a few years of mind-altering perception under his belt with the Tibetan monks. Back then, he told me he yearned to live a life with eyes wide open, and the monks there had welcomed him in. I had no doubt that at some point, he would return to them. I fully expected after everything that had gone down, for him to bow out of the studio. It didn't fit anymore, from what I knew of him. So that morning, I had called Julie. She had been with me since the beginning, helping with the day-to-day running of the studio. I had her take over the management and told her to reach out to our contacts for alternating master classes for the next few months. I had yet to tell Tsui.

When he stood and took center stage, he sent me a wink. "I have thought long and hard regarding how I feel things should play out. I have conversed with both Adam and Laughlin, and they have asked me to share my choice and why. As you have shared this adventure with us and in some way are all part of the Templar mystery, we will vote on my suggestion."

He paused and looked at each face in the room in turn and then began with the Templars' history. "What we started out as is not what we became. Through necessity, our roles as protectors changed, and we were no longer guarding people, but their fortunes as well. In retrospect, it makes perfect sense, as no one would want to travel with their fortune strapped to their back. I believe the order was at risk when they became a bank. I have always found it odd that the Catholic Church, which holds infinite treasures' worth of fortunes, never came under the same scrutiny as the Templars. Be that as it may, when we became moneylenders, we made the same mistake as the Jewish moneylenders, allowing kings to borrow to the point of never being able to pay back. And when that happened, incredible forces were lined up against us."

After a brief pause, he went on. "Scotland and parts of England gave Templar survivors free passage here, and it was widely accepted that the Templars have ceased to exist for the past seven hundred years, but we know that isn't true. Here in this room, stand some of the most influential leaders of the Templar factions. But it is time for that to be laid to rest."

Tsui took a sip of his drink and cleared his throat before continuing. "If we hide the treasure, then Scotland, and specifically Laughlin's and Adam's lands, will always be in danger. Fortune seekers will inevitably end up here. If we dig and give our secrets to the world, I believe a catastrophe will occur. I'm not saying that is a bad thing, only that we are not yet ready for something of this magnitude to take place. So here is my suggestion. We move the treasure to Tibet, deep into the mountains, with no association with the Templar Knights or Masons or any other group. The sheltered monks will ensure its secrecy. Believe me when I say that is not all that is hiding deep in the mountain range. I chose this because it removes the families from the spotlight, removing our knowledge of the location. Once it's taken, not even I will know the exact location of the hiding spot. In other words, ladies and gentlemen, there is no going back. Once the decision is made, it is final."

The room remained quiet while we all chewed on Tsui's idea.

Finally, he said, "Let's put it to a vote. Those in favor, raise your hands. Now, those against, raise your hands." The only person to raise their hand the last time was Lenore.

"Lenore, are you opposed or asking a question?"

"Well, I'm uncertain and need clarification." Lenore turned toward her older sister and asked, "You're okay with this?"

"Yes, one hundred percent. I would like to have a life that doesn't involve being shot at."

"But don't you think it is dishonoring our father and what he stood for?"

Suri's gaze hardened. "I hope to never honor what he stood for. He used me as leverage, lied to me, and treated me like garbage my entire life. If you got to hide at home, for the most part, go unmolested in your daily life, then I'm excited for your lack of experience. On the other hand, my children would bear the burden, and for what, Lenore? So we could claim a heritage that has no peace. If the world needs a new banking system, then I wish them luck. With Laughlin at the helm, I'm sure we can navigate life without the Templar stigma hanging over our heads. And my advice to you is to go and live. Stop being such a good girl, Lenore, and live your life."

I'd never heard Suri talk like that before and wondered if it was Laughlin's influence or just last night's events. Her father had been killed, after all, but not before trying to kill her first.

Tsui spoke. "Again, all those in favor, raise your hand." This time everyone raised their hands, and I blew out a relieved breath.

"Excellent, Geoff will assist me in making the arrangements, and thank you. I believe this is the right thing to do."

Tsui and Geoff left for a more private spot, while the rest of us broke off at that point into small groups.

Suri and Laughlin approached us.

"Have you two decided what to do?" Before I could answer, Malcolm spoke. "Yes, after making funeral arrangements, O and I are going on a trip. We are heading to Ireland, then Amsterdam, Holland, Barcelona, Spain, Bruges, Belgium, Budapest, Hungary, and for the final leg of our trip, Italy. You two care to join us?"

"Wow," Suri said, a huge grin painted on her face. "How exciting, O." We squealed with joy and jumped up and down like kids.

"How about it, brother, want to join?" Malcolm asked.

"How about we meet up with you in Italy? I have plans for Roswell and want to spend a little more time with Adam before leaving for home, which will help me get things started. It's time I took notice of the world closest to home and made a difference."

Suri gazed at Laughlin lovingly. "I can't wait to help," she said, earning her an appreciative look.

"When we get back, we will make some changes too. I want to go to New York and see the studio business that O has built up and bring some of that knowledge back here and to my other locations in Europe. Then I will be ready," Malcolm said.

"For what, Malcolm?" He gazed at me with such intensity, I felt a blush spread across my cheeks.

"To settle down, and for you to say *I do*. To make babies and live happily ever after."

"I see. And if I'm not ready?"

"You will be, lass. I can feel it."

"Okay."

"That's all beautiful, O, just okay?"

"Yes, I trust you, Malcolm." He kissed me, and the promise from earlier was infused with need this time.

"Excuse us, we need to ahem, do something... now." We left the room to chuckles from Suri and Loc.

Chapter 20

Malcolm

Partings and endings, beginnings and changes. The next few days were a whirlwind of goodbyes with our Canadian friends. Ace, Alex, Adam, Otter, Montana, Geoff, Eddy, and his crew flew home the same morning we made our way back to Roswell.

According to him, Declan had met the love of his life in Skyla. He was staying in Scotland for a bit to spend some time with her and his mother. Tsui had managed to negotiate the terms of release for Declan's missing friend, Charles Muir, who was on his way home to Edinburgh. Declan had a lot to celebrate, and the Scotsman walked around with a permanent grin on his face. Now that we knew each other, I had no doubt we would see more of the Highlander.

Everyone who had attended the wedding was going home, except my father. I missed him already, and I know Laughlin did too. He'd been like a second father to him, and despite what he'd done near the end, I still loved him and would remember the good times.

The six of us drove home, but we were far from the same people we'd been a week ago. Lenore, usually demure and filled with dimpled enthusiasm, was quiet in the back seat. Marcus was deep in thought beside her, and I wondered if something happened between the two during our stay at the castle.

Beside me, O held my hand and watched the scenery outside the window. She was happy, and it showed on her face. In the front, my brother spoke enthusiastically about his plan and where he was beginning. Suri threw in the occasional word of encouragement as he talked about Roswell.

Marcus and Laughlin had been best friends for years and lived close to each other. So when Marcus declined the dinner invitation for later that evening, Laughlin seemed surprised. All eyes inadvertently traveled to Lenore, who was keeping her eyes on the ground.

Marcus left, and Lenore went inside.

Suri and O exchanged troubled looks.

"If you need me, Suri, just call. Something isn't right with those two," I told her.

She nodded and gave me a hug. "Are you two sure you don't want to stay? It's going to be weird going home and finding no one there. You are our family. Please stay if you wish."

I wanted to, I really did, and I knew O was good, either way. I looked at my brother, who surprisingly embraced me and held me tight. I allowed my defenses to drop for a rare moment as I took comfort from his strength.

"I'll take care of everything, brother," he uttered in my ear. "I'll call you tomorrow with the details, and please, bring your woman back tomorrow to visit with my wife. If you're up for it, I could sure use your help before you leave."

I pulled back. "Of course. We'll see you tomorrow for lunch?"

Suri sighed in relief. "Lunch would be great, and if you two are busy, O and I can spend some lagoon time with Lenore."

"Oh, how I do love your lagoon, Laughlin." O sighed as if she had just seen Heaven.

"Is that right? Well, then I will build you one, lass," I responded."

"But then I will have no excuse to visit my bestie when I want."

"Yeah, brother, why not build a tennis court? I don't have one of those."

We all laughed. "See you tomorrow, and thanks again, Loc, for taking care of the details."

He waved me off like it was nothing, and for him, it probably was. He'd buried his mother and his father. I was his only family left, well, and now Suri. My heart was hurt for the birth father I never knew, for the birth mother who had used me, and most of all for Henry. He'd been a wonderful father to me.

When we arrived at my home, that sounded weird. I took O on a tour. I felt like I was in a museum. I'd never felt like this was my home, and now it felt even more foreign. "Laughlin was right, O, this place feels like a ghost town. So big and cold and filled with spirits of the past. We should remodel. I don't think I can live here. I was never particularly fond of it in the first place."

"Where do you feel at home?"

"Any bed that has you in it."

"I really liked that bed we slept in that Adam designed. Did you order one?"

"I didn't, but I will. Can I ask you, now that you have seen all fourteen thousand square feet, what would you do to the place?" We were standing in one of the long, dark hallways.

The place was four hundred years old, and I swear it still had the same finishings.

"I would move or remove a few non-essential walls, to allow in the natural light from the windows. You know me, I'm all about the light. I would take some of the smaller spaces and create bigger ones. I would do a floor-to-ceiling wall bank of glass along the south side and out there, on the other side, is where I would put our outdoor space. Except, with all the rainfall, I would make it indoors and create a vast glass enclosure. I would add a workout room and a space for you, you know, a home gym. I would take the southwest corner and add a sunroom off the kitchen, and this would be a yoga and plant space. Speaking of plants, this incredible opening you have that goes right to the roof, I would put in windows and grow a garden right in the center of the house, so it had lungs. Then I would take that massive nursery, cut it in half, and update the bathroom."

I listened, amazed at her ideas.

"Oh, and renovate the master bathroom to include a sauna. I think that's about it. Light, air, and space, with a few refinements. As far as the décor goes. I would keep many of the antiques and add some bohemian accompaniments and some leather, to give this a nice blend of old and new."

"Wow, you already know what you would do, so do it," I said.

O turned a shocked look on me. "What do you mean?"

"Simply that I am making you a project manager. You can start now, or when we get back, totally up to you."

"But I don't know anything about residential renovations, and I certainly wouldn't know where to source them here."

"Well, you are in luck. My brother is about to get started with creating a workers' union for Roswell, and as we are in the district, our house can be the first project. Adam is lending him bodies to get started. He's even putting in a second manu-facturing location for those massive beds."

"Really, then we'll need six."

"That many?"

"Of course, there is ours and four guest rooms, and when our children are bigger, they will need them too."

"Aren't you full of surprises?" I pulled O in tight, kissing her softly.

She moaned, "Yes, I suppose I am."

"Come, lass, we need to initiate my bed."

"Ugh, I'm sure it's seen plenty of action."

"No, O, I have never brought a woman to my home. I told you, every single sexual experience has been a one-night stand. You are my first and only woman."

"In that case, take me to bed, handsome."

I lifted her and carried her up the stairs to my suite, then flung her into the center of the bed and pounced on top of her. "Hello, little girl."

O's pupils dilated, her breath coming out in short pants. "Hi," she husked.

"I wanted to compliment you on your good behavior. I guess my message in the woods was received."

Her facial expressions altered and morphed several times. "Yes, sir," she gulped.

Oh god, she was so damn perfect. My cock was straining inside my pants, and there was no doubt O could feel it pressed against her belly.

"Tell me, little one, what do you want?"

"Whatever you wish to give me, sir."

"Tsk tsk, now you're bad. Answer me, O, what do you wish for?"

"For you to make me forget everything except your body taking me to the edge and pushing me over, time after time, until the world is gone and I forget my name. I want you to make me crawl and beg and take every orifice in my body as it sings with your invasion. Take me, Malcolm, like there is only today, only now, and only us."

"That's better, little yogi. Now get ready, 'cause here I come." I yanked her pants down and brought her knees up in one swoop that left her breathless. I pressed her knees toward her ears. Her flexibility allowing me to open her wide.

"Don't move your legs."

I dipped down and licked her glistening folds. She spasmed under me with the shock of my tongue invading her. I smacked her juicy opening, and as she squealed, I bent my head down and licked again. Her body spasmed, responding with every stroke of my tongue and the gentle slap of my hand.

"O."

"Yes, Malcolm?"

"Are you looking to get your ass spanked?"

"Uh, maybe."

I was glad she couldn't see my face as I silently laughed. She was such a brat, and I loved that side of her too. "Okay, brat, time for a spanking." I pulled away and then yanked her over my lap. She kicked half-heartedly, like putting up a little fight would disguise how wet she was and how badly she wanted it.

Keeping her over my knee, I grabbed my hairbrush from my end table—something she hadn't had yet. By the time I was done with her, she wouldn't remember her own name.

Looking up, I realized that quite unwittingly, I'd set us up in front of a mirror. Enjoying the view of O's perfect ass, I changed her position and pulled her onto one thigh, and allowed her to rest her chest and head on the bed. Then I wrapped one of my legs around both of hers, to keep her still. I loved this pose because her parted thighs allowed for a perfect view of her arse and channel opening.

I brought the brush down with a crack and watched in the mirror as a cherry red mark showed up. Below me, I heard a whoomph of air release from O's lungs. I brought the brush down several dozen times until she stopped screaming and squirming. When she hung limply, still in position, I removed my leg from around hers and spread her legs wider. She was so wet that my pants beneath her were soaked in her pleasure.

I watched, fascinated, as I ran one finger from her gloriously hard clit to her anus. I heard a guttural moan as O arched her back and looked for friction on her needy button. I rubbed her juices all around her tight bud and slid in a finger. With my other hand, I alternated and watched as she worked herself into a lather. Finally, I began to pump her hard and fast with both hands, and she climbed and crashed so many times, I lost count. My entire pant leg was now drenched as were my shoe and sock. I decided that when we renovated, I wanted mirrors at all angles so I could watch her beautiful body respond to me.

When I could take no more. I stood and placed her on the bed on her knees. I wanted her to feel her spanking every time I thrust into her and my pelvis hit her hot ass. Pushing her chest down, I entered her in one hard thrust. O released instantly, and I could hear her babbling. This made me smile, incoherent, I believed she asked for permission. I pumped her hard until I released. The hot jetsam sent O spiraling off one more time.

I pulled out of her when it was time and held her in my arms. "How was that, beautiful?"

"Exactly what I asked for and more." She smiled in happy exhaustion.

"Malcolm."

"Yes, love?"

"Just that. I love you."

My heart caught with her words. "I love you too, O, and I promise that I will forever."

"I know, sexy man, and I will hold you to your promise."

"I've no doubt in my mind you will."

"Malcolm."

"Yes?"

"Thank you for making all my pieces make sense and for loving all of me."

"No need, lass, you did the same for me."

The End

Skylar West

Skylar West is a Canadian writer, new on the author scene and making a big impact with her steamy romance books. She loves walks in the rain, hot cups of delicious java, overly large sweaters, and the type of steamy sex she writes about in her novels. A cat lover, this author looks forward to writing many more novels.

Find her on Facebook: https://www.facebook.com/sky.west.1806

Don't miss these exciting titles by Skylar West and Blushing Books!

Sons of Sicily series
His to Learn
His to Train

Crown and Cross series
Laughlin
Malcolm

Angels and Demons Series
Fallen Angel
Dark Angel Discovered
Dark Angel Awakened
Dark Angel Rescued
Dark Angel Redeemed

Single Titles
The Dark Side of Kingsley

Anthologies
12 Naughty Days of Christmas 2020

Blushing Books

Blushing Books is the oldest eBook publisher on the web. We've been running websites that publish steamy romance and erotica since 1999, and we have been selling eBooks since 2003. We have free and promotional offerings that change weekly, so please do visit us at http://www.blushingbooks.com/free.

Blushing Books Newsletter

Please join the Blushing Books newsletter
to receive updates & special promotional offers.
You can also join by using your mobile phone:
Just text BLUSHING to 22828.

Every month, one new sign up via text messaging will receive
a $25.00 Amazon gift card, so sign up today!